DEATH
OF THE
RIVER MASTER

Also by Allana Martin

DEATH

OF THE

RIVER MASTER

Allana Martin

Thomas Dunne Books
St. Martin's Minotaur ⚜ New York

THOMAS DUNNE BOOKS.
An imprint of St. Martin's Press.

DEATH OF THE RIVER MASTER. Copyright © 2003 by Allana Martin. All rights reserved. Printed in the United States of America. No part of this book may be used or reproduced in any manner whatsoever without written permission except in the case of brief quotations embodied in critical articles or reviews. For information, address St. Martin's Press, 175 Fifth Avenue, New York, N.Y. 10010.

www.minotaurbooks.com

Map by James Sinclair

Library of Congress Cataloging-in-Publication Data

Martin, Allana.
    Death of a river master / Allana Martin.—1st ed.
        p. cm.
    ISBN 0-312-30685-7
    1. Jones, Texana (Fictitious character)—Fiction. 2. Mexican American Border
Region—Fiction. 3. Women detectives—Texas—Fiction. 4. Presidio County
(Tex.)—Fiction. 5. Texas—Fiction. I. Title.

PS3563.A72319D47 2003
813'.54—dc21

                                                                      2002191956

First Edition: July 2003

10   9   8   7   6   5   4   3   2   1

Author's Note

The legal system of the United States is based on English common law, in which each case may be considered unique and each decision may be based on prior decisions in other courts. Thus the outcome of any given case is unpredictable.

Mexico's legal system is based on Roman or Napoleonic law, called the Napoleonic Code. Violations are listed in law books (codified). Extenuating circumstances play no part. Instead of jury trials, a judge oversees the collection of evidence, determines guilt or innocence, and hands down a sentence. A judge's declaration that a person is a probable suspect may be appealed even as the prosecution unfolds. There is no bail, no writ of habeas corpus, no plea bargaining, no probation, no early release.

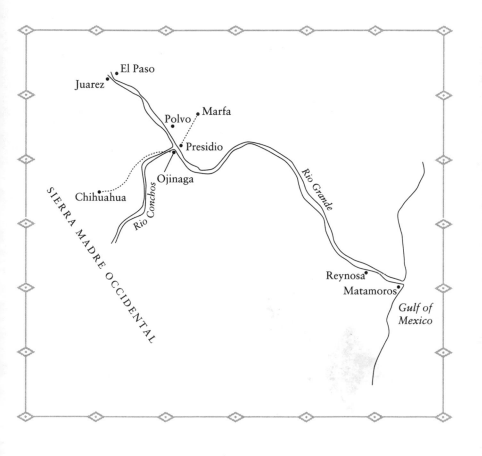

How can life on the border be other than reckless?
You are pulled by different ties of love and hate.

—GRAHAM GREENE

Laredo, Nogales, Tijuana, and other towns along the
U.S. border had become international cities that—
much like the city-states of medieval Italy—often had
more in common with their counterparts across the
border than with their respective capitals.

ANDRES OPPENHEIMER,
Bordering on Chaos

DEATH
OF THE
RIVER MASTER

PROLOGUE

Border Patrol agent Luis Ruiz popped a jalapeño in his mouth and Crosse Hickman deliberately made a gagging sound. Luis chewed hard and swallowed, his big face reddening.

"Twenty bucks says he can't keep it down," Crosse said good-naturedly, earning appreciative laughter from the crowd of ranchers, agents, and locals who stood around the table where the two men sat. Each opponent had started with a plate of fifty hot green peppers and was now down to the last few.

Crosse, a young man with his long brown hair tied back in a ponytail, winked at his girlfriend, Nina, then put a pepper in his mouth, chewed briskly, swallowed a mouthful of beer, and gulped down the fiery mass.

Luis picked up the three remaining jalepeños, bent his head back, opened wide, and dropped them into his mouth.

He chewed with luxurious slowness, swallowed, then leaned back in his chair, folded his arms, and smiled. "Your turn."

Nina patted Crosse's back and whispered encouragement in his ear. He took his time, drank some beer, ate a cracker, then selected the largest of the three peppers on his plate. His eyes watered as he chewed and his forehead beaded with sweat. With a weak grin, he looked down at the last two peppers, let out a long sigh, and shoved the plate away.

"Victory to Luis!" someone shouted.

The crowd clapped, the other Border Patrol agents slapped Luis on the back, and I brought bowls of ice cream as an antidote.

Bet money was changing hands when the bell jingled as someone opened the front door. A small-statured, boyish-looking young man came in and stopped still, staring around him with a lost look, as if shocked by the presence of so many people.

"Too late, Daniel," Crosse shouted. "You missed it . . . Jeez, why the long face? You look like somebody died."

"My father," Daniel Mehendru said numbly.

"What?" Crosse said, his face wiped of the silliness of the moment. "Oh, man, you're serious, aren't you. I'm sorry, I'm so sorry."

The crowd drew back into itself, made sympathetic murmurs and put away their money. A gray-haired Border Patrol agent took Daniel's elbow and steered him to a chair at the table, where he slumped down limply. Crosse jumped to his feet and went to put a hand on his friend's shoulder. Nina moved to Daniel's other side and knelt by his chair.

I fetched a cup of coffee and set it in front of him. "What happened?" I asked gently.

"He was murdered," Daniel said, looking at the cup of coffee as if he'd never seen one before. "In Ojinaga. The sheriff called me this morning. Somebody shot Dad Saturday night while he was sitting in his pickup." Daniel took a deep breath

2

and looked up at Crosse. "I came to ask if you'd go with me to get the . . . my father."

"Sure thing, man," Crosse said.

Daniel shoved his chair back and got to his feet. Standing beside his friend Crosse, he looked tiny, almost delicate, his light brown eyes wide with disbelief and shock. Crosse and Nina kept him between them as they went, as if he might fall down without their support.

After the doors closed behind the trio, Luis asked for a bottle of Pepto-Bismol. I got one from behind the counter. He drank straight from the bottle.

Rancher Vernon Hyde handed me a twenty for the contestants' beers. "Too bad for the kid," he said, "but I'm only half surprised somebody killed the River Master. Zanjiv Mehendru was a first-class troublemaker."

"He's made his last trouble, now," someone behind Vernon muttered as the group broke up and started out the doors.

ONE

Friday, April 12

If you don't hurry, Texana," my husband called from the other room, the bridge will be closed by the time we get there."

I held the neck of the red knit top wide and pulled it over my head, stepped into the matching skirt, and zipped up.

"It's only five-forty," I said, running a brush through my gray-streaked black hair.

"And we have a ninety-minute drive in front of us," Clay said, coming into the bedroom, jingling the pickup keys in his hand.

Tall and slim, he wore a neutral linen jacket over a pale blue open-necked shirt and brown slacks. He'd polished his best pair of calfskin boots until they gleamed. His close-cropped white hair emphasizes his tan skin and green eyes.

"You look handsome," I told him.

It isn't often that we get to dress up. We practically live in work shirts and jeans. I own Texana's Trading Post, where we also live, near the end of Ranch Road 170, which runs forty-eight miles from Presidio, Texas, on the Rio Grande, northwest to Polvo, a tiny community two miles beyond my place. Forty feet behind the trading post is Clay's veterinary clinic, serving all of Presidio County, since he's the only veterinarian in the county's nearly four thousand square miles of huge ranches. Everything here is miles from nowhere.

I grabbed my jacket from the bed and slipped it on. Summer's heat had arrived in March, but the desert nights remain cold well into May. As we walked through the great room of our private quarters in the rear of the trading post, Jefe barked, thinking she was going outside with us. Jefe is a long-haired, cinnamon-colored Chihuahua we inherited from a neighbor now serving time at a federal penitentiary near Dallas for drug smuggling.

Our other and older pet is Phobe. The bobcat had been barely grown when we got her from a family with four small boys. She'd been named inadvertently by the young mother, who'd remarked to her husband, within the hearing of the boys, "Get rid of it. I'm phobic about having a wild animal in the house." Her youngest son had picked up on only a part of one word, hugging the baby bobcat and saying, "Phobe, Phobe, kitty is Phobe."

Now the full-grown, twenty-pound bobcat stared up at us, her great round eyes scornful because we were going out. Phobe thinks it's her right to participate in all our activities. I stooped to stroke her head, but that didn't lessen her resentment at what she considered our desertion as we left.

Clay drove my '99 white Ford supercab rather than put more miles on his dented green Chevrolet pickup, which gets rough use serving the big outlying ranches that make up eighty percent of his veterinary practice. We were going to Ojinaga for dinner with our friends Mario and Olivia Berrera.

The early evening sunlight diffused the ever-present dust into a golden haze, softening the brown-and-dun landscape. The Chihuahuan desert has two seasons, winter and summer. Spring's only herald is the south wind that hurls itself against the sierras, bringing with it the summer's heat.

Our end of the river road is a landscape of rock scree and thorny plants, offset by the narrow greenbelt of mesquites and swaying salt cedars on the brushy riverside.

This landscape changes at Presidio, which sits at the junction of Mexico's Rio Conchos and the boundary we share, the Rio Grande. The surrounding river plains had been farmland since before the Spaniards arrived in 1534. They still would be, except for the prolonged drought. The Rio Grande, shared by Texas, Colorado, New Mexico, and Mexico, is drained by heavy agricultural, municipal, and industrial use. It arrives at El Paso already diminished. The malquiladora industry of Juarez and El Paso's thirst uses up the rest. Not for nothing is our section of the river—from El Paso to Presidio—known as "The Forgotten River." No river at all would be more accurate.

Presidio hugs the wide bed of the once great river, a cluster of one-story buildings. It has more streets unpaved than paved, a few brick homes, many more built of cement block, and a population of five thousand. Most of the businesses sit along O'Reilly Street, which is dominated by Santa Teresa Church. The fenced Border Patrol compound and the school system provide most of the jobs.

We followed the pavement to the port-of-entry bridge, the only legal crossing for four hundred and fifty miles, though there are plenty of illegal ones. With the river now only a memory, any point is a crossing.

Like Presidio, Ojinaga is low-built and colored by alkali dust blowing in from the desert. The town of forty thousand sprawls over a low hill and runs out into the desert. Ojinaga's physicians were once experts in gunshot wounds. They regularly treated victims of the territorial wars among rival narcotraficantes who drove the streets with their gunmen waving semiautomatic weapons. The drug trade still flourishes, but the men behind it have learned to go more quietly. Random gunfire still happens, but more often it is the bribe, not the bullet, that persuades. It helps that the drug cartels have much of the army, the federales, and the judiciales on their payroll. This is the reality of life in la frontera.

Ojinaga and Presidio are separated by a bridge, but united by a culture. Border Spanish is our language; citizens on both sides of the river likely have aunts and uncles, cousins, or sweethearts on the other; both towns celebrate the Fourth of July and Mexico's independence day, the Sixteenth of September. Many families in Ojinaga, using the addresses of relatives, send their children to school in Presidio. Most people shop for groceries, clothes, furniture, and appliances in Presidio and visit the doctor, dentist, and druggist in Ojinaga. Strangers to the borderland often ask who we are. "Fronterizos," we answer. We live in a world apart, where everyone treats everyone else as an equal and the mode of life is set by the heat of the desert and the crosscurrents of the politics of two countries.

Clay drove slowly down Avenida Libre Commercio toward the far side of town. The streets were busy, people gossiping in doorways, teenage girls congregating like bright parrots, boys standing in bunches, doing more staring than talking. The preventivos, traffic cops, were on the busiest street corners to yell down stop-sign and red-light violators. Uniformed and equipped at their own expense, few had cars, though I noticed two bicycles parked at the curb.

Our destination was Cuchara's Restaurante, famed for its seafood, which is driven in weekly from Tampico by an auto hauler who owns the wrecking yard that takes up most of the block around the corner and across the street from the restaurant. He hauls out stolen cars and trucks, returning with the seafood, which he keeps in a freezer compartment fitted into the back of his rig's cab.

Like all Chuchara's regulars, we bypassed the parking lot for street parking. The lot is paved with chopped strips of asphalt roofing, which not only softens in the heat of the day and sticks to your shoes, but also contains some of the original roofing nails. The man who lives across the street makes a living repairing the punctured tires of new customers. We found a parking space around the corner near the end of the block and walked back. All along the street Texas license plates outnumbered the orange-and-black Chihuahua State plates.

"I hope we can get a table," Clay said, as he pushed open the bright purple door of the restaurant.

TWO

Beyond the purple door, the interior of Cuchara's is equally colorful. The long narrow room has twenty-foot ceilings painted midnight-blue with golden stars. Ceramic cherubs in mock gold leaf hang in the corners. The walls are covered in murals depicting Ojinaga's history, from the arrival of Cabeza de Vaca to the invasion by Pancho Villa's revolutionary forces on Christmas Day in 1913, which sent much of the population fleeing across the river to Presidio, thus beginning the cross-border family ties of the two communities.

The restaurant was crowded. Our friends the Berreras beckoned to us from a table near the center of the room. Mario, a gray-bearded man with the beginning of a paunch, stood to greet us, kissing my cheek and giving Clay a two-armed hug with much back-patting.

Mario has been our dentist for fifteen years. His wife Olivia owns the bakery on the plaza. Our relationship with them shifted into friendship after Clay saved the life of their chow dog. Emperor Ching's kidneys were slowly failing and Clay arranged for a transplant. Unable to bring the dog into the country legally in time to save him, Clay and my friend Pete Rosales carried the sick animal across the river on the footbridge Pete had built so that he could walk across, even when the river flowed. I met them on the other side and we drove from there to a private landing strip, where a local rancher flew Clay and Ching in his private jet to Davis, California. There, in an operating room at the University of California campus, Ching got a new kidney from a donor dog. Six days later, Clay and a recovering Ching made the return journey.

"We just launched the bottle of tequila," Mario said to us, speaking over the noise of the jukebox that played old 45 rpm records from its place by the kitchen door. Mario poured the golden liquid from the tall bottle into small, double-handled shot glasses and passed them to us. A bowl in the center of the table was filled with fried tortilla strips, glistening with residual grease. I ate one so the tequila wouldn't land on an empty stomach.

We didn't need menus. Cuchara's seafood night has only one specialty, that being the choice of the chef and owner. Mando Jimenez is very loyal to his regular customers and comes out of the kitchen to greet people, sometimes sitting down at a table to gossip. He wears a big smile and an apron that doesn't bear looking at. Mando believes in good conversation as well as good food and encourages lingering over meals.

"I was afraid we were going to be sitting in the dark," Olivia said. "That windstorm last week took down a power line. The electricity came back on this morning."

"Too bad the wind didn't blow in any rain," Clay said.

"Gracias de Dios that I'm not in a business that depends on the weather and the water supply," Olivia said, touching the gold cross at her neck.

"The water situation is dire," Mario said.

"Zanjiv Mehendru understood that," Olivia said. "He was a good friend to Mexico."

Clay shot me a look that said, "Too good a friend," but we stayed away from the touchy subject of whether the late head of the United States Section of the International Boundary and Water Commission had been right to side with Mexico over its refusal to honor its treaty with the United States. Mexico refused to release water from reservoirs in Chihuahua State into the Rio Conchos, which enters the Rio Grande just above Presidio. Mehendru's public comments about Mexico having the greater need had so angered local growers that they'd scathingly referred to him as the River Master, a nickname that had stuck.

"What's the latest on the murder investigation?" Clay asked.

"Six weeks since Mehendru was shot and still no arrest," Olivia said. "You know the policía called in the judiciales," Mario said, pouring another round of drinks. "According to *La Voz de Ojinaga,* the judiciales have questioned over one hundred people. The authorities are becoming embarrassed. Mehendru wasn't just anyone. Televisa did a Twenty-Four Horas segment on him just a few months ago."

"Have you heard," Olivia said, "that he had a common-law wife living here?"

"Mercedes Solar. The *Presidio International* mentioned her in the story about the murder," I said. "It seems that she and Mr. Mehendru showed up at the courthouse in Marfa one day last November and signed a declaration of informal marriage."

"I never heard of such a thing," Olivia said.

"Neither had the county clerk. According to the paper, Mehendru had to tell her the page reference in the Texas Family Code. He was right, of course. That's what so many people found irritating about him. He was always right."

"Like with the Marfa golf course," Clay said.

"What about it?" Mario asked, splashing tequila into our glasses once more.

"Last year," Clay said, "when the levels in Marfa's city wells dropped nearly ten feet, the city council passed an ordinance restricting lawn watering. In a couple of weeks, when the wells dropped another two feet, the council banned watering. Then a bunch of kids went up to the municipal golf course one night to do a little beer drinking. They were sitting on a blanket in the middle of the third green when the sprinklers came on and soaked them. Turned out the city was watering the golf course three nights a week. At the next council meeting most of the town showed up to complain. The members told the crowd that the greens were being maintained with treated sewage water, not water from the city wells. Zanjiv Mehendru didn't live in Marfa, but he reads about all this in the newspaper and the very next night he slips onto the golf course, checks out the system, and finds the water is being pumped straight from the wells. The next day, he calls the newspaper. The council had to issue a public apology."

Mario laughed and poured another round of tequila.

"This was a good thing Commissioner Mehendru did," Olivia said, "publishing the truth."

"He was known for it," Clay said, raising his glass.

Conversation stopped as a skinny waiter carrying two large trays arrived at our table.

"Mando's outdone himself," I said, tasting the small red snapper stuffed with crabmeat seasoned with garlic and onions.

As we ate, we touched on other border topics: the manufacturing plant that would be coming to the Presidio Industrial Park, which meant jobs for Ojinaguenses; the Cross-Border Nature Preserve Project, a planned seven-hundred-thousand-acre conservation area being funded by a private company in

Chihuahua; the Ojinaga narcotraficante wanted in the United States and kidnapped by the judiciales, who transported him across the river, handcuffed him to a tree, and made an anonymous telephone call to the Presidio County Sheriff's Office giving the location. Popular opinion in Ojinaga held that the state police had been paid by a rival drug smuggler.

Mario signaled the waiter, who came with the tray to remove the empty plates. He was taking our dessert orders when six hard-eyed men in dark uniforms, shiny badges pinned front and center on their baseball-style caps, walked in.

They stopped at the front and stood surveying the room. An old man, whose job it was to sit by the jukebox and make change, reached down and unplugged it. Conversation, service, and eating stopped. The six men wound their way between the close tables like a thick-bodied snake and stopped at our table. One, a big man with eyes so dark the pupils didn't show, placed a hand on Clay's shoulder.

"You have some identification, señor?" he asked.

"Yes," Clay said, reaching for his wallet.

Before he could remove his driver's license, the man grabbed the wallet from his hand, glanced at Clay's driver's license, and grunted. The wallet vanished into his pocket.

"We have an order for your arrest," he said coldly.

"I don't understand," Clay said.

"He doesn't understand. Show him."

Two of the others moved in, yanked Clay to his feet, and handcuffed him. The tables between us and the door emptied as diners scrambled out of the way.

"This is preposterous," Mario said, getting to his feet.

The two policemen spun Clay around and marched him toward the door, kicking chairs aside and toppling tables as they went. I moved to follow them, but Mario held me back.

"There's nothing you can do. They won't let you talk to him," Mario said hopelessly.

"Listen to him," said an anonymous voice from another table.

"We have to try," Olivia said, getting up to come with me as I shook off Mario's hand and headed after my husband.

THREE

Olivia and I reached the narrow sidewalk in front of the restaurant in time to see the judiciales shove Clay into a Jetta van. He glanced back and saw me.

"Call Lisa Wharton," he shouted over his shoulder.

The judiciales climbed in, slammed the doors, and the van sped away.

"Wharton. Is that your abrogado?" Olivia asked.

"Lisa's not a lawyer. She's a small animal vet in the next county over from us," I said. "Clay's worried about his practice."

"He'd do better to worry about himself," Mario said.

"Do you know any abrogados here?" Olivia said.

I shook my head.

"We'll go see Enrique," Mario said. "Give me a minute to go back inside and pay." He left us. Olivia asked where I was parked.

"Around the corner."

"You can follow us to Enrique's house," she said.

That's when I remembered that Clay had the keys.

I left Olivia to wait for Mario alone, telling her I'd meet them at my pickup. I rounded the corner and crossed the street to the wrecking yard. It was getting dark and the street had no lights, but I could see well enough to make my way through the rows of rusting vehicles to the squat, tin-roofed building at the back with its solitary lighted window.

A few feet from the door, I called out, "Hola, señor."

A wide man passed by the window and opened the door. The autocamiónero had a face as round as a full moon. He wore a beige shirt intended to fit loosely on a man of lesser substance, red knee-length shorts that squeezed his massive thighs like biker's pants, and yellow rubber thongs on his curiously small feet.

"I've locked myself out of my pickup," I told him. "I was hoping to borrow a slim-jim."

He looked at me assessingly, then said, "I'll pop the lock for you."

I know how to use a slim-jim. I keep one at the trading post for the occasional customers who lock their keys in the car. I assumed the man wanted to make sure I didn't walk off with his, so I merely said, "Thank you."

He drifted forward on those tiny feet like some kind of flotation device. I followed his slow, gliding movements to his rig, parked behind the house on a dirt drive that opened onto the next street. A big, hungry-looking dog chained to the bumper leaped and snarled at our approach. The hauler barked "Silencio," and the animal whined and ducked its head, the heavy chain clanking against the ground.

The autocamiónero opened the cab door, climbed up, reached in, and stepped back down with a long metal rod in his hand.

It took him two minutes to pop the lock. I gave him the five-dollar bill I had in my pocket. He eyed my pickup.

"Four-wheel drive?" he asked.

"Yes."

"How old?"

"Five years."

"How many miles?"

"Too many," I said.

"Insured?"

"Yes."

"You decide you want a new one, leave it here any night," he said, turning to go. "Be sure to leave the keys in the glove compartment with the papers."

It took me only a moment to hot-wire the pickup, something my father had taught me, and a very handy thing to know when you live in the backcountry.

As I sat up and got behind the wheel, Mario and Olivia pulled up beside me and slowly passed. I cut on the headlights and pulled out, following them into the heart of town.

In the middle of a long block, Mario slowed and pulled in behind a red Nissan Xterra parked at the curb in front of one of the houses that lined the street and opened directly onto the sidewalk. I parked behind the BMW and checked my watch by the dome light. Fifteen past nine. The port-of-entry bridge would close at ten.

I got out and stood behind Mario and Olivia on the narrow strip of cracked cement. The heat of the day had vanished with the sun and I shivered in the wind. Down the block, someone had left a door open, sharing light and ranchera music with the neighborhood.

The building's heavy wood door had no bell. Mario knocked. A handsome young man in a knit shirt and chinos opened the door. "Don Mario! Doña Olivia!"

Mario said, "Texana Jones, may I introduce my godson, licenciado Enrique Vera."

"Welcome to my home." He shook my hand, hugged Mario, brushed Olivia's cheek with his lips. "Come in, please." He moved aside to let us pass and gestured us ahead of him down a tile-paved hall that opened straight into a book-lined room with a desk and a single lamp burning. Four creased vintage leather chairs surrounded a marble-topped pedestal table littered with newspapers and magazines. The walls of the room were hung with prints of works by various Mexican artists from the forties and fifties, as if the house had belonged to his grandparents and his law practice was too new to pay for updated furnishings.

"Señora Jones is from Polvo, on the other side," Mario said. "A small problem has arisen here requiring a lawyer."

"I'll treat your problem as if it were my own," Enrique said. "Please, let's all sit down." He waited until I was seated, then said, "Tell me."

"We . . . my husband and I, were at Cuchara's with your godparents when the police came in and arrested Clay."

"The judiciales," Mario said.

Hearing that, Enrique nodded solemnly and sat up straighter. "What's he supposed to have done?"

"They didn't say, they just took him," I said. "Clay hasn't done anything. It's a mistake."

"Of course," Enrique said. "The policía may detain someone for three days only, but the judiciales have more, shall we say, discretion. Has your husband had an automobile accident, perhaps? Maybe someone was injured who seemed okay at the time, but later fell sick or died. No one would have expected you to remain at the scene, of course, but someone might have taken down a license number."

"No," I said. "Nothing like that."

Enrique stood up. "Let me make a call and see if I can find out what's going on." He left the room.

"Enrique is a very smart boy," Olivia said, as if to comfort me.

I sat silent, listening to the sounds of the street: the roar of a motorcycle shifting gears, laughter from somewhere down the block, all against the background of the neighbor's radio.

As the minutes passed, Olivia patted my hand from time to time. After ten minutes, Mario said reassuringly, "All will be well. You'll see."

Finally, Enrique returned. He stopped in the doorway. Our eyes rose to his face. He looked somber.

"What's wrong?" Olivia asked.

The young attorney avoided my eyes. "The situation is a bit difficult. Señor Jones is being held for the murder of Zanjiv Mehendru."

FOUR

It was nine-fifty when I said good-bye to Mario and Olivia outside Enrique Vera's house. I made the bridge at one minute to ten, paying the toll as I left one side and stopping at the customs booth before I crossed to the other. The agent, commenting that I was cutting it close, nonetheless asked me the obligatory questions: "What is your nationality? Are you bringing in anything?" I answered, then was on my way.

Beyond the bright lights of the bridge and the few lights of Presidio, darkness enveloped me, the black of the night cut only by the high beam of my pickup's headlights and the black fear I felt for Clay and into which no light shone. I lost all sense of time and distance as I followed the long-familiar route of the undulating pavement, so when the headlights hit the mud-colored adobe trading post I was shocked to find myself home. After nearly a year and a half of living in it, the soft lines of the structure still seemed new to me, like arriving at someone else's house.

In 1888, my great-grandfather, Franco Ricciotti, had bought six hundred and forty acres of land here on the Rio Grande. He built the original wood-frame building the same year. Like my grandfather and father before me, I'd grown up in the old building and lived there all my life except for four years of college and one year of a first marriage when I'd lived in Dallas, a suffocating experience that had nearly killed me. Then, in a few hours one night, a fiery propane explosion had destroyed the cottonwood-beamed building and every memento of my past life. Clay and I lived in a borrowed RV while adoberos from across the river constructed the new trading post on the site of the old. When the building was finished, Clay and I borrowed a cattle trailer and drove to Chihuahua City to buy tables, chairs, and beds from an old man who crafted them from mesquite wood. A side trip to Chihuahua's Wal-Mart provided us with blue glass dishes, white bed linens, and pillows in yellow and red and blue. Gradually, the new trading post was becoming a home, and the more familiar it became, the less I missed the old.

As I pulled up close to the back door, I caught the glow of two round eyes that blinked and vanished. Phobe had an inmate sense of timing and would have expected us home much earlier, so she'd been sitting on the blanco beneath the window, watching and waiting for our return.

As soon as I walked in, Phobe pounced on my ankles with both big front paws. Jefe barked shrilly, tail wagging furiously. I made soothing noises as I petted them. After they calmed down, I made coffee. The caffeine wouldn't matter, I was too worried about Clay to sleep.

I cut on the outdoor security light and took my coffee with me across the graveled back lot to Clay's clinic. The converted trailer house he'd used since our marriage had been badly damaged by the heat of the flames and the shrapnel of debris rocketed in all directions by the propane explosion that had destroyed the trading post.

The new clinic was adobe, with a small waiting room, a bigger office with plenty of shelves for his reference books, a nice examining room, and an operating area. The adjacent kennels and pens for housing and observing sick animals had been repaired and left as they were. Tonight the kennels were empty, the puppies Clay had been treating for a severe case of mange had been picked up by the owner yesterday. I recorded a message on Clay's answering machine referring emergency calls to Lisa Wharton's number in Alpine, then I called Lisa's voice mail and relayed the information that we had an emergency and Clay had asked her to stand in for him for the next week. Lisa would take all small animal calls and any large animal emergencies. Before I left the clinic, I checked Clay's appointment book for the day that Zanjiv Mehendru had been murdered. I could hardly forget the date. The local weekly, the *Presidio International,* had run one story after another, incremental advances in the scant facts of the case.

Flipping through the pages for late February, I found a notation for Saturday, the twenty-third: "Impaled bull-Barton's." I remembered the case because Clay had been so pleased that he'd been able to save the animal. "Barton" referred to Barton Howard, my father's contemporary and a lifelong fronterizo. A better, more reliable witness to Clay's whereabouts couldn't be found. Best of all, Barton's call had come in late afternoon, and his Curling A Ranch was upriver, more proof that Clay couldn't have been anywhere near Ojinaga that night. I'd had to keep his dinner warming in the oven because he'd come home so late. He'd been worn out and had gone to bed immediately after he ate.

Back in the kitchen, I topped up my coffee and carried it to the couch. Phobe leaped to my side and flopped down with her back hard against me. Jefe jumped up on my other side and climbed on my lap. I twisted around and put the cup of coffee on the table behind the couch so I could stroke the dog's silky coat, getting as much comfort as I gave.

Among the many baby animals we'd raised I recalled a newborn raccoon that someone had brought in. Clay had tended it for months, keeping the tiny, dependent creature under a heating pad and feeding it every few hours, night and day. When it was old enough to be allowed outside, Clay had walked it at night so it would learn to forage for food.

It was unthinkable that anyone could believe Clay capable of murder. I tried not to imagine what he might be enduring at the hands of the judiciales by concentrating on what I had to do.

If the prison warden would let me, I'd see Clay tomorrow. Make that later today. It was now 2:00 A.M. Enrique had promised to go with me to try and ease my way at the state prison and hopefully speak with Clay himself, but we didn't know if we'd be allowed to see him. The lawyer thought there was a chance that Clay might be released after questioning. The police had, after all, questioned many people about Zanjiv Mehendru's murder. Clay might be just one more.

My coffee had cooled, but I drank it anyway. Jefe fell asleep in my lap; Phobe gave a deep sigh and relaxed enough to put her head down on her paws. As soon as it was a decent hour for an early riser like Barton Howard, I'd telephone.

I wanted to telephone my father, but it was too early. He lives with a dog, a tame coyote, a cat, and a few longhorns on the three-thousand-acre ranch left to him by my mother. He suffers from severe depression and I've spent a lifetime trying to protect him from stress, but not from reality. He's deeply fond of Clay and would want to be told.

I roused the dog and bobcat so I could get up to take a hot shower and get ready for the rest of the day. Phobe loves water and tried to get in the shower with me, but I nudged her out. She sat on the bathroom floor and pawed at the water drops she could see running down the inside of the shower curtain. Jefe pranced nervously around the bathroom, her nails clicking against the tile floor. I towel-dried my hair and pushed it into place with my hands, then slipped on a robe and went out to pack some things Clay would need if he had to stay in prison a week.

Phobe and Jefe came to sit in the middle of the king-size bed and watched as I rolled three pairs of shorts, three pairs of socks, two clean work shirts, and two pairs of jeans into a neat bundle and put them together at the bottom of a white garbage bag. Phobe swatted at the tennis shoes I placed on top and tried to chew the laces. A baseball cap and five handkerchiefs went on top of the shoes.

I went to the front of the trading post for unopened packets of other things Clay would need: soap, dental floss, toilet paper, razors, shaving cream, a package of Handi Wipes, toothpaste, toothbrush, a tin of Altoids, a bottle of ibuprofen, a comb, and a plastic mug.

That left me with nothing else to do but worry. I set the alarm for six and stretched out on top of the bedspread, thinking as I did so that I should have flipped the sign on the front door to CLOSED, in case I forgot in the morning, but I was too weary to get up. Phobe and Jefe had already commandeered the pillows on Clay's side. I closed my eyes, trying to relax but not expecting to sleep.

The last thing I remembered was Phobe's soft snoring, then the alarm rang. After I shut it off, it was a long minute before I stopped listening for the sounds of Clay in the kitchen cooking breakfast. Then the enormity of what had happened came back to me.

I made coffee and fed Phobe and Jefe. The dog gets a half cup of the all-natural dried dog food that Clay orders for Jefe from Munster Milling. Phobe gets a half pound of chopped horse meat and vitamins. I scrambled an egg and had a second cup of coffee, then telephoned Barton Howard, silently giving thanks that he'd finally, at age seventy-two, put in a telephone.

"I just wanted to make sure that I had the right date for Clay's visit to you," I told him, after I'd explained why I needed to know.

"I've got the canceled check right here in my desk. Hold on a minute." I could hear him rummaging among his papers, then he came back on the line. "The twenty-third of February. That's the date. I wrote out the check right there on the spot. It was after dark when Clay finished stitching the bull. I offered to grill us both a sirloin and open a bottle of Val Verde Lenoir, but he said you had his meal waiting. Those fools, arresting Clay for that man's murder."

"Thanks, Barton," I said, warmed by the indignation in his voice for what was happening to my husband.

"What time are you leaving for Ojinaga?" Barton asked.

"Eight-thirty. The lawyer said there was no point in getting to the jail before ten-thirty."

"I can be at your place by eight to go with you."

"Barton, that's so good of you, but there's no need. They may not let me in to see Clay."

"Okay, but I'm here anytime you need me," he said.

I made four chicken sandwiches and put them and a six-pack of bottled water and six candy bars into a Styrofoam container, then went to the get dressed. Twice, I ignored knocking at the front doors. At seven forty-five, tired of waiting, I locked up and left.

Halfway to Presidio, at the point where the mountains on either side of the flood plain fold back to let Radio Ojinaga's signal through, I tuned in to catch the news. The reader was announcing that the judiciales had arrested a nortéamericano for the murder of Commissioner Zanjiv Mehendru. So much for the hope that they might let Clay go.

FIVE

Saturday, April 13

How strange that a day can alter one's feelings toward a place. I am a fronteriza born and bred, crossing the river as casually as some drive to a mall. Now, I felt alien in my own world, the bridge a barrier I was hesitant to cross.

On the way to El Cereso, the state prison where Clay was being held, I passed expensive homes that—despite the drought—boasted lush green lawns, moved on through streets where scattered stores displayed sparse inventories in dusty windows, and finally through several blocks of crumbling adobes. The only color here was the bar opposite the prison gates, convenient to the just-released and the prison guards. It was a bright red, almost perfectly square little building, its single screenless door propped open by a gaudy ceramic pig, its name proudly painted in white foot-high letters across the front: LA BOLA DE ORO, The Pot of Gold.

The prison had cement-block walls and a high chain-link fence topped with loops of razor wire. I parked across the street at the end of the block, in front of a statuary lot selling cast-concrete replicas of Venus de Milo, fountains, and saints. I was early. The street was empty of cars and activity. It was Saturday, the day for socializing, shopping, and soccer. In the heart of the town, the plaza would be overflowing with street vendors selling breads, fruit ices, tacos, and shoe shines, but around the prison block life seemed suspended. I sat with a nervous stomach and waited.

Forty minutes later, during which I'd resorted to reading the paperback I'd brought along for Clay, a red Nissan turned the corner, pulled off the uncurbed street, and parked on the dirt. Impeccably dressed in a dark blue suit, Enrique Vera looked confident as he approached my pickup.

I replaced Clay's book in the bag with his clothes and toiletries, grabbed the handle of the cooler, and got out.

"I spoke with the warden this morning," Enrique said after we'd greeted each other. "You'll be allowed to see Clay for five minutes." My face must have shown my dismay, because Enrique immediately explained. "That's the normal visiting time on weekdays, five minutes at ten and two. The warden is making an exception, letting you in on a Saturday. Sundays and Wednesdays are family days, with two-hour visits. You can come back tomorrow at eleven."

I nodded. Seeing my husband briefly was better than not seeing him. "Radio Ojinaga announced the arrest," I told Enrique. "That means they don't intend to release Clay."

"Yes, I heard it, too," Enrique said. "Let me carry that for you." He took the cooler from me.

The gatekeeper, with a holstered gun fixed to his belt, rolled back the heavy prison gate, its bars painted an incongruous kelly green. He handed me a clipboard. I signed my name, wrote in the date and whom I was visiting.

While Enrique did the same, I looked around the prison yard, a thirty-by-thirty box with graffiti-covered walls. The heat rose in waves from the cracked-cement pavement, carrying with it the stench of urine. Four black-uniformed guards leaned their backs against the high walls of the compound, a fifth squatted in a triangle of shade in one corner, a rifle resting across his knees. A sixth perched on the roof.

The gatekeeper took the bag from my hands and the cooler from Enrique and carried them to a table inside a flimsy wooden gatehouse that did little more than provide shelter from the sun. Inside, a radio played loudly, romantic songs of love and loss in Spanish. The gatekeeper searched through the contents, pausing to open a can of aftershave and sniff the fragrance. Finally, satisfied I had nothing contraband, he brought out both cooler and bag.

"The water isn't allowed," he said. Enrique folded some cash into the gatekeeper's breast pocket and the gatekeeper passed me the bag and cooler, then called to a guard standing in a nearby door. The guard disappeared inside, only to return in a few minutes and motion for us to come forward. We followed him into a hallway with tan paint flecking off in large patches. A short, stern-faced man with a large silver belt buckle shining in the middle of his sharply pressed black uniform stood in an open dooray. Draped across his sloped shoulders was a short-haired white tomcat with one blue and one green eye.

"Warden León Martinez?" Enrique said as we approached. The man with the cat gave a curt nod. Enrique removed a card from his wallet and presented it to the warden, then introduced me. I set the cooler down to shake hands.

"I'm grateful to you, Warden Martinez," I said, for letting me come to see my husband today."

"You understand," the warden said in an abrupt tone, "this is an unauthorized visit. And only you, señora. You, señor, must wait in here." Moving on soft feet, in order not to dislodge the cat, the warden went to the next door and opened it. Enrique glanced at me, I nodded, and he left us. The warden closed the door, spoke to the guard in an undertone, then moved into his office. I retrieved the cooler and followed. The room was no bigger than twelve-by-twelve and held a desk with a telephone and two chairs, and an elderly man in a wheelchair being spoon-fed by a shaggy-haired, middle-aged man in brown pants and a green-and-red-striped shirt with the sleeves rolled up.

"That's my father," the warden said. "He doesn't know who he is or where he is anymore, so I bring him here with me each day. Some of the prisoners, like Chido here, earn food money by taking care of him. He'll be done with his breakfast in a minute and Chido will wheel him out to the yard."

The thin old man had only white stubble for hair. He slumped in the chair, his bony old hands crossed on his lap. As each spoonful was lifted to his toothless mouth and pushed in, he swallowed mechanically, his face showing no pleasure at the taste of the mashed beans.

"I thought it best," the warden said, "to have your visit here in my office." As he sat down at his desk, he lifted the cat from his shoulders with one hand and deposited it on the desk, where it rolled on its back. I set the cooler on the floor, took the other chair, and watched the prisoner Chido as he wiped the old man's mouth, put the empty bowl and spoon on his lap, and wheeled him out. Shortly afterward, there was a knock, then the guard ushered in Clay. He looked at first wary, then astonished when he saw me. The warden waved away the accompanying guard.

Clay's green eyes were bloodshot, his hair uncombed, and his face unshaven. His clothes were rumpled because he'd slept in them. But he gave me a look that said he was okay.

The warden stood up and said, "Five minutes." As he reached for the cat, it sneezed.

"How long's he been doing that?" Clay asked.

"Nearly a month."

Clay approached the desk and looked the cat over, head to tail. "Does his nose run?"

"Sometimes it drips."

"He has an allergy," Clay said. "I could prescribe something that would stop the sneezing. I'm a veterinarian."

The warden held the cat with both hands and said, "See, behind both ears, where he's scratched the skin raw? This worries me more than the sneezing."

"What's his name?" Clay asked.

"Zapata."

"Hello, Zapata," Clay said, rubbing the cat's shoulders while he looked in its ears. "He has ear mites." Clay rubbed the tip of his little finger inside one of the animal's ears, causing the cat to complain loudly. "See that?" he said, holding his finger up.

"Dirt?"

"Droppings from hundreds of tiny bugs living in his ears. My wife can bring some medicine for Zapata's ears as well as for his allergy," Clay said, stroking the cat's back.

"I would be grateful," Warden Martinez said. He made a grab for Clay's hand and shook it in both his. "Come, Zapata," he said, going to the door. The cat jumped from the table and ran out. The warden beamed at me and said, "Ten minutes," before he closed the door behind him.

"You bought us five extra minutes by paying attention to the cat," I said to Clay.

"I hate to see an animal miserable."

"I hate to see you miserable."

Clay came over, put his arm around me, and kissed the top of my head. "How are you holding up? That's what's important. I'm fine, except I don't have a clue what's going on."

"They haven't questioned you?" I said, reluctantly pulling away from his arm to look him in the eye.

"The cops brought me straight here from the restaurant without saying a word. I asked to see the arrest order they claimed to have. I might as well have been singing in the shower for all the good it did. I don't know why I'm here."

"You're being held for the murder of Zanjiv Mehendru."

"What!" He went over to the chair and sat down hard, gripping the seat with both hands as if holding himself down. "I didn't even know the man except by reputation. I think I waved to him once on the road."

"You have a lawyer, Enrique Vera. He's the Berreras' godson. He came with me today, but the warden wouldn't let him see you."

"You think it will come to that? I'll need a lawyer?"

"Clay, I've already checked the date of the murder. You were at Barton's ranch all afternoon and evening."

"The bull that tried to jump the fence. I remember."

"And after that, you were home. You ate and went to bed."

"Then they'll have to let me go," he said.

"It's just a matter of going through the formalities. Enrique thinks you'll get a hearing in five or six days."

"Five or six days!"

"When he presents his evidence. Well, they can't have any, can they?"

"No," Clay said tentatively, "but they arrested me. They must think they have something."

"Enrique thinks it's some bureaucratic mistake. Probably they're just going through the motions of holding you for a hearing to save face."

While we talked, I'd been clutching the plastic bag of clothes and bath items so tightly that my hand hurt. I dropped it onto the desk. "Here's fresh clothes and some other things. And I brought food," I added, turning to get the cooler box and setting it on the desk. I opened it, lifting out one of the sandwiches. "Have you had anything to eat since last night?"

"Not a bite," he said, making an effort to smile. I unwrapped the sandwich and opened a bottle of water for him. His first bite or two was perfunctory, but after that, hunger took over. He finished the sandwich and ate a Snickers before asking if I'd called Lisa.

"I left a message. I'll talk to her today as soon as I get home."

"If she can't stand in for me, call Kevin Haynes in Odessa. He owes me a favor."

The door opened. The guard waited. Clay stood up.

"I'll be back tomorrow," I told Clay. "Sunday is family visiting day. We'll have two hours together."

He shook his head. "I don't think you should come. I don't like the idea of you being in this place."

"It makes me feel better to see you."

"It makes me feel better to know you're safe at home. They might decide to arrest you, too. You never know. This whole thing is crazy."

"I have to bring the medicines for the cat."

"Okay," Clay said, after some thought. "He'll need chlorpheniramine tablets and Cerumite." He stood up and took off his jacket and handed it to me. "You can take this to the cleaners." He picked up the bag and the cooler, then paused. "Have you told Justice about all this?"

"I'll call Dad when I get home, but don't worry, this will all be over soon."

Clay nodded as if agreeing, but he didn't sound optimistic when he said, "Besides the cat meds, bring some roach spray and Lysol for me."

SIX

Enrique waited for me in the hallway.

"It was a good visit? Señor Jones is well?"

"All right for now," I said.

We followed the guard out of the shabby hallway and into the sun. After the barred gate banged shut behind us, we moved away from the prison walls and across the street to my pickup.

"What did the judiciales ask your husband?"

"Nothing."

Enrique shrugged. "Even the judiciales like their weekends off."

"You'll let me know if you find out anything," I said, unlocking the pickup door.

"I'll try to get through to the attorney general's office in Chihuahua on Monday to find out who'll be handling the case. That will give us a better picture of how things stand."

"Will you talk with Clay tomorrow?"

Enrique shook his head. "The prosecutor has to give the okay on that. I thought it was worth a try, coming along today, but . . . let's don't worry until we know what we have to worry about."

"Clay was on a call the night Zanjiv Mehendru was murdered," I said, explaining about the emergency at Barton Howard's ranch. "That puts Clay over sixty-five miles from Ojinaga with a witness who'll back him up. The rest of the night, he was home."

"This is good. I'll take a written statement from Señor Barton and from you."

"We haven't discussed your fee," I said.

"Please, you and Señor Jones are gente de confianza of my godparents. My fee will be small, six hundred dollars through the hearing."

"And if this goes beyond that?"

"I have faith that it won't."

I knew he was telling me what I wanted to hear. All I could do was hope that he was right. We parted and I got into my pickup. The wind was rising with the heat of day and a coating of dust already veiled the white paint, turning the Ford tan. I took off my suit jacket and hung it over the headrest to keep it from wrinkling, fastened my seat belt, started the motor, and turned on the air conditioner.

The drive home seemed to take forever and I felt more lost and separated from Clay with every mile that passed. Only one other time in my life had I felt so frustrated by my inability to help to any purpose.

When I was twenty-one, my mother dropped dead of an undiagnosed heart condition. I came home from college to find my father locked in his study, where he remained for weeks, shut in with grief magnified by his chronic depression. I was terrified that he'd kill himself. Nothing I did or said seemed to make a difference. I cooked meals and left them on a tray outside his door. He ate so little, I lost eight pounds in empathy. I'd packed away all my mother's belongings and was debating whether I could go back to the University of Texas to graduate when he emerged, unable to cope with anything more than basic living. He closed the trading post, told me to go back to school, and moved to the ranch. Eighteen months later, with a diploma and my divorce papers from a college-romance marriage, I returned home to find that my father had signed the trading post and the accompanying section of land over to me. I haven't been away from home since.

Trying to banish the thought, I cut the radio on and listened until the mountains blocked the signal, but there was nothing new beyond the report of the arrest. So far Clay hadn't been identified by name.

When I got home, a blue pickup was parked in front of the trading post and a plump woman with tightly waved black hair sat in one of the chairs on the front porch.

I parked next to Claudia Reyes's vehicle. Even before my door opened, she was on her feet asking me if everything was okay. For a moment I thought she must know about Clay, then I remembered why she was there. "Claudia, the meat! I forgot. I'm so sorry."

I was storing fifteen pounds of shredded fajita beef in my commercial freezer for Claudia. She and her husband Ruben run Casa Azul Restaurant, open only on Friday and Saturday nights, out of the front room of their home. Beyond a standard refrigerator, Claudia hasn't any storage, so I keep many perishables for her and in return she supplies me with home-cooked flour tortillas and tamales.

"No harm done," she said. "I was worried about you. It's not like you to close on a Saturday."

"There's been a little problem," I said, echoing Mario's words last night to Enrique.

"Is that a Mexican poco problema?" she said, eyeing me with the knowledge of old friendship.

Claudia wasn't being nosy. Our part of the world is about

as far from the rest of Texas as you can get. Presidio County is bigger than some states, but it has a population of less than ten thousand, and that's counting those passing through. Not minding other people's business can be tantamount to neglect.

"I'll tell you about it while we get the meat out of the freezer," I said, unlocking the front door.

Claudia followed me, trailed by Phobe and Jefe.

"Is it too late?" I asked dismally, as we removed three rock-hard packages from the freezer shelf. I'd promised to have the meat thawed when Claudia came to pick it up.

"Not to worry," Claudia said. "My customers can eat cheese enchiladas. Now sit down and talk to me."

We put the meat on the kitchen counter and sat at the long stainless-steel-topped table that economically served as prep and dining space. I poured out the story of Clay's arrest. As I talked, Claudia's mouth tightened and a deep frown creased her forehead.

When I'd wound down, she patted my hand. "Have you had lunch?"

"No, but I—"

"I'm going home and give the meat to Ruben, then I'm coming back with some food for you."

I was so grateful I didn't even make a token protest. After she left, I changed into jeans, a white cotton T-shirt, and sandals, then I telephoned my father. His voice sounded firm and strong, a sign that he was having a good day. I could hear Woo Hoo, his lovable brown-and-white dog, barking in the background.

"Dad, something's happened here. We're okay, but . . ." I didn't try to sugarcoat what had happened. My father may suffer from depression, but he's too intelligent to appreciate being patronized. He let me tell it straight through.

"You satisfied with this lawyer?" he said.

"He seems to know what he's doing."

"You think he's got enough influence that anybody in the

Chihuahua attorney general's office will listen when he talks?"

"I don't know," I said.

"Well, I'm sorry this is happening to you and Clay. He's going to be released, but don't sit on your hands. Start finding out all you can about what Zanjiv Mehendru was doing in Ojinaga. Besides visiting that woman of his."

My father may live a hermit's life, but he knows what goes on in the borderland through an old-boy network, men like Valfre, the traveling barber who crops his hair once every six weeks, ranchers on both sides of the river for whom he did survey work in the years before his illness, and old friends he grew up with, like Barton Howard.

I knew my father was right. Things weren't over and I couldn't afford to assume the end was in sight.

SEVEN

I put the OPEN sign in place and cut the fuel pumps on. In five minutes, I had two customers pumping diesel for their duallies. After they left, I telephoned Lisa Wharton's office. Her young assistant, Karen, answered the telephone and put me on hold for seven minutes. This was only the beginning of what promised to be a big bill month for my long-distance carrier, and only last week I'd gotten a card announcing rate increases.

Just when I was considering hanging up, Lisa Wharton's chirpy voice came on the line. "I got your voice mail and I'm good for next week. Clay's not sick, I hope?"

I told her the truth, because if the news was on Radio Ojinaga, it wouldn't be long before the media got Clay's name from the authorities. Then, everyone would know. At that moment, Claudia came in the back door carrying a tray covered with foil. Whatever was under it smelled so good that my mouth watered and my stomach growled. I told Lisa I appreciated her help and would be in touch as soon as I knew anything more about when Clay might resume his practice.

Claudia had set a place for me at the table. She placed the tray in front of me. "Sweet corn tamales seasoned with chopped green chilies. Made fresh this morning."

I picked up my fork and took a bite. The ground cornmeal wrap was tender and moist, the filling sweet and spicy. Claudia had even brought a glass of iced tea with a slice of fresh lime.

I'd finished one tamale when the bell on the front door jingled as a customer came into the trading post. I put down my fork, but Claudia said, "Stay. I'll wait on them."

In a minute she was back. "Natalie Pacheco wants to know if tonight's movie is okay for Pablo to see?"

I choked on a bite of tamale. When I stopped coughing, I said, "It's a Western." Scary movies gave Pablo nightmares.

I looked at the kitchen clock and decided I was brain-dead. Three fifty-nine on a Saturday, and if Pablo Pacheco's mother hadn't come by, I'd have sat there the rest of the afternoon without setting up for Movie Night. A few months earlier, I'd gone to a garage sale in Marfa to pick up clothes for resale. Instead, for ten dollars, I'd come home with a large box of used videos, mostly early Hollywood Westerns, like *Arizona Gunfighter* with Bob Steele as Colt Ferron. Although I do a modest business in video rentals, after I went through the box and saw what I had, I decided few of my customers would pay a three-dollar rental for them, but they might come to see them for free, so Movie Night was born. Show time was six o'clock. The kids enjoyed it so much that I'd decided to keep it up through the summer.

Claudia came into the back and insisted on taking over from me at the sink, where I was washing her plate and glass.

"You know, Texana," she said, "because of what happened to my cousin Oscar, I understand better than most what you're facing. I can arrange with his wife Jesusita to cook Clay's meals."

Four years ago, Claudia's cousin, an Ojinaga taxi driver, had been held for the murder of a German tourist who'd been found dead in the backseat of his cab. He'd been released after the real killer had been discovered, but by then his family had spent much money trying to free him. It was a reminder I could have done without right now.

"Thanks, Claudia. Probably, I'll go in each day until the hearing. It shouldn't be too long."

Her look said, "Don't count on it," but her words were kind. "It'll do him good to see you. Keep his spirits up."

After she'd gone, I went to the storeroom and got out the folding chairs and set them up for the adults who accompanied their kids to see the movie. The kids themselves preferred to sprawl on the exercise pads I'd bought for very little from a San Angelo gym that was going out of business.

Feeling grimy after the prison visit and the dusty drive home, I showered, then fed Phobe and Jefe. Both ate the way they always did, gobbling down the food as if they were in a race to see which one could finish first. At five-fifteen, I microwaved a quantity of popcorn, drizzling half with a blend of melted butter and chili powder, the other half with salt and butter, and put the big bowls out on the counter in front. Lastly, I got out the night's video and put it by the tape player next to the big-screen television my father had given us for a housewarming gift when we'd moved out of the RV into the new trading post.

At twenty minutes until show time, the first of the movie audience arrived and I hurriedly went to shut Phobe and Jefe in the bedroom. Most children are intrigued by the bobcat and want to play with her, not realizing that a bobcat's idea of play includes powerful teeth and claws. As for Jefe, she stands only eight inches high and weighs less than three pounds, too fragile to be underfoot.

When everyone was settled, I turned off the lights and started the movie. The kids, including eight from Providencia, a village three miles on the other side of the river, sat cross-legged on the pads right in front of the television, feeding popcorn into their mouths without their eyes leaving the screen. For some, mine was the first television they'd seen, the movies the only ones they'd ever watched. The corny dialogue, grainy images, and flat color entranced them.

Two hours later, *Gunfighters of the Plains* ended. The grandfatherly man who'd driven the kids from Providencia stayed to shop. I helped him load his groceries, then waited until his ancient pickup squeaked out of the parking lot, kids bouncing in the back end, before turning off the front light.

I released Phobe and Jefe from the bedroom. While they played I folded the chairs, rolled up the pads, picked up scattered kernels of popcorn, and changed the trash bag. I was so sleepy, I felt cross-eyed. I went to the kitchen, ate a bowl of cereal, giving the leftover milk in the bowl to Phobe, and went to bed. It was five to ten. Phobe and Jefe tumbled onto the bed together, taking the pillows on Clay's side.

A muffled crash and snarling woke me at 2:00 A.M. I knew exactly what the noise was. For the second night in a row, I'd forgotten to bring in the bird feeder I'd hung in the mesquite by Clay's office and the raccoons had found it. Let them tear it apart. I was too tired to go out and scare them off so I could bring the feeder in. I tried to go back to sleep, tried not to think about Clay. Sixty wakeful minutes later, I put on a heavy robe and thick house shoes and walked out to sit on the front porch.

The air was crisp and cold. There were no lights in view, no visible sign of humankind, nothing except the dark shadows of the trees along the river and high above them the blacker forms of the Sierra Bonita Range on the other side. Higher still, stretching the full length of the horizon, a wide ribbon of cloud looped the night sky, five brilliant stars sparkling through its sheer veil.

I dropped my eyes and saw a humped form scurry across the parking lot in a line to the river. One of the marauding raccoons. The varmints are opportunistic eaters, going after grubs, fish, roots, berries, mice, my birdseed.

Opportunistic. Had the judiciales been opportunistic in arresting Clay? Had they so needed to solve a well-publicized crime that they simply picked someone out? It had happened in Juárez to five bus drivers, arrested for the rape/mutilation murders of a number of young women who worked in the malquiladora plants. A Juárez magistrate had sentenced all five to prison. They were there still, though more young women had been raped, tortured, and killed in the same horrific manner.

I gave the cold night one last shivery look, then rose and went inside to try and sleep.

EIGHT

Sunday, April 14

Normally, I close the trading post on Sunday, but today I left the OPEN sign in place to accommodate anyone who might have missed me the day before and need necessities, like gas or food. My customers adapt easily, routine being something we don't follow much out here. Ranch and rural life can hold surprises that frustrate any regular course of action: a calf strayed miles from its bawling mother, an axle broken on the ranch road that hasn't been graded in a while, an ankle twisted in a fall from a horse spooked by a rattler. Things like that can shoot routine all to hell. That's the way my plans were when Hugger Baines showed up looking for Clay.

I hadn't finished my second cup of coffee when he drove his white Chevrolet pickup across the parking lot and straight around to the back. He was knocking on the clinic door when I came out to explain that Clay wasn't here.

"Where's he gone, then? I sure need to find him. One of my mules is down a sinkhole."

Hugger's nut brown face was streaked with sweat, his shirt and jeans were dirt-smeared, his boots scraped down to raw leather in several places. He could be anywhere in age from fifty to seventy, but now he looked beaten down.

"Clay's in Ojinaga," I told him.

"Monk's been down there all night," he said, as if that explained everything.

"Monk's the mule?"

"He was coming out of the top pasture down to the corral when the ground fell in under him," Hugger said. "He's mired up to his shanks. I dug all night to make room to get a tarp under him. Now I need a winch and another pair of hands."

"How far is your place?" Clay had been to Hugger's many times over the years to doctor one animal or another, but as it happened, I'd never gone with him.

"Sixteen miles, by the road," Hugger said.

I thought about it. The trading post wasn't Hugger's closest neighbor, but except for one ranch that had a resident manager, he was surrounded by thousands of empty acres. As neighbors go out here, I was it.

"I'll get Clay's pickup keys and follow you."

Ten miles below the trading post, we turned north along a track that traces the path of Panales Arroyo. It was a slow six miles ending at an abandoned adobe at the narrow mouth of a side canyon.

Hugger stuck his head out the window and shouted back at me, "Just a ways more."

Ahead, I could see two lines of bent grass and traces of bare earth where the tires of his pickup had eroded the ground on his trips in and out.

The track climbed, but the pitch was easy. The air was growing cooler and the sky overhead was a perfect blue. The yellow blooms of prickly pear and the red blooms of strawberry cacti dotted the canyon walls. We reached the bowl-shaped upper canyon. Here bear grass and juniper replaced the drier landscape. I barely had time to notice the house, small and square and built of stone, and a corral, from which six mules steadily observed us, before Hugger was out of his pickup, pointing, and gesturing for me to follow.

I drove at a snail's pace after his lean figure. Fifteen feet from the sinkhole, he held up a hand. I stopped, then turned the pickup and backed in so we could use the winch to haul Monk out. As soon as I cut the motor, I heard the song of canyon wrens.

"It's me, Monk. I'm back. We're gonna get you out, old son," Hugger was saying as he knelt over a depression in the earth. I edged over and took a look. The animal had fallen front-feet first and his rump was high. The mule couldn't get any purchase to help us leverage him out. I could see his wide back and the back of his neck, but although the animal's ears pivoted in the direction of Hugger's voice, the mule couldn't turn his head. The earth around him, where Hugger clearly had been digging, looked crumbly. Off to one side was a pile of rough-cut rectangular rocks.

"Was this an old well?" I asked.

"Looks like it. There's a spring about a mile above."

"Is that where you get your water?"

"Yeah, I pipe it down to the corral and house," he said, getting up from his knees. "I already got a tarp under Monk. After I hook up the chain, you handle the winch while I steady the old boy."

"You going to get into that hole?" I said. "If that mule panics and starts thrashing around, he could kill you."

"Never been around mules, have you," Hugger said. "They're nothing like horses. A horse steps into trouble, he panics and tries to run, whether it helps or hurts him. A mule gets into trouble, he stops and thinks, 'Why am I in trouble and what's going to happen if I move?' Monk's been down there all night, so he's had plenty of time to think. He knows he can't get out by himself. He knows he needs help."

Not being the familiar of mules, I couldn't argue with that, so I manned the winch and hoped Hugger was as smart as he thought Monk was.

It took us four tries to free Monk: once to get him used to the feel of the pull against his belly, again to reposition the tarp when we got enough lift that Monk's angle of incline allowed the tarp to slide up under his hind legs, a third to get his front legs level with the rest of him, the fourth to get him on solid ground. Once there, he stood still until Hugger unhooked the tarp from the chain, then trotted away toward his friends in the corral. Hugger went after him to open the gate. I followed.

"Does this little canyon have a name?" I asked Hugger, as we rinsed our hands in the water trough.

"Choke Canyon, 'cause it's nearly closed off down there at the neck where we came in."

I dried my hands by shaking them and wiping them down my jeans. The view down the little canyon was magnificent, a trickle of green ribbed in by raw rock walls crowned by allthorn shrubs.

"I guess you don't get many visitors up here," I said.

"Didn't used to," Hugger said. "When I first bought this place from old Pedro, there wasn't a soul come by from one year to the next. Not like lately. You'd think being this far out would discourage folks."

Hugger was one of our in-comers. He'd shown up eleven years ago, saying he was retired from the Forest Service and looking for ranch work. A family named Mellows hired him. Eventually, Hugger married a teacher from Presidio. Three years later, she died of cancer and left him her savings, which were considerable, since, although teaching doesn't pay much in Presidio, there's not a lot to spend it on, either. Hugger used the money to buy the eleven sections from an old man who wanted to go back to his home village of Guadalupe Bravo to die.

"I wouldn't think anyone could find you that easily," I said.

"Three visitors in as many months," he said.

"That's a lot of company all the way out here."

"It is. The first was some journalist, a kid about twenty-five, wanting to do a story on the hermit of Panales Arroyo. I asked him who that might be and he said it was a man named Bugger and did I know him. I told him I did not and sent him on his way. It wasn't a week later that the second one showed up. I was fixing a leak in the pipeline when a woman in one of those little bitty Toyota pickups bounced up the canyon and stopped right at my heels. Said she was with some environmental group, I forget the name, and did I know my mules were despoiling—she actually used that word—the landscape for native species."

"What did you say to her?" I asked.

"Oh, I told her I appreciated her input, but that the only native species I knew about were cougars, bobcats, porcupines and skunks, and that the first two liked mule meat, and that the mules let the other two strictly alone. Of course, that got her nose all out of joint. No sense of humor, these crusader types. She carried on about my donating the place to her group. When I said no, she had what my grandmother used to call a hissy fit. Said she'd have this place declared a unique environment zone and get rid of me and my mules. She left in a huff. When the guy with the ponytail showed up a few weeks ago, talking about a nature preserve, I figured she'd sent him to argue with me. But he was polite, even after I made it clear I wasn't interested in selling."

Just then, the mules set up a commotion. Hugger said they wanted feeding. He thanked me graciously for helping him rescue Monk. I told him, without exaggeration, that I'd enjoyed myself.

"Come back and I'll introduce you to the rest of my mules," he said. "Distinct personalities they have."

I started down the canyon, looked at my watch, and felt slightly sick. It was five after ten. I was an hour from home, I needed ninety minutes to get to Ojinaga, I hadn't prepared Clay's lunch, and I smelled mightily of mule.

NINE

It seemed to me every part of Clay's old pickup rattled as I drove down the narrow canyon in what had to be record time.

At the trading post, I ignored the pleadings of Phobe and Jefe to play, washed only the body parts that showed, zipped up clean jeans so fast that I caught my panties and had to rip them free, slapped together four ham sandwiches, hurried out to the clinic to get the cat medicines, then to my pickup. I was almost to Ojinaga when I realized I'd forgotten the Lysol and roach spray Clay had asked for.

In Ojinaga, trucks and cars overflowing with passengers cruised the streets around the plaza in the Sunday ritual of paseando, seeing and being seen. The traffic cost me the precious minutes I'd gained in my teeth-rattling drive down Ranch Road 170. It was twelve forty-six when I reached El Cereso. I'd get to see Clay for fourteen minutes. This time we didn't meet in the warden's closet-size office, but in the prison yard. Some sixty prisoners and their relatives, including children, milled about the hot space, like guests at an over-crowded party. Family Day. A few people sat on upside-down buckets arranged like conversation areas outside each cell. The unlucky men who had no visitors leaned against the cement-block walls or lay on the dingy sponge mattresses inside the windowless cells and smoked, watching the family groups through squinted eyes.

"I thought something had happened to you," Clay said, coming to meet me as I crossed the prison yard.

"I'll explain while you eat."

When we reached the eight-by-eight cell, I handed him the sack of food and nudged a nearby bucket with my toe.

"Don't sit on that!" he said. "We use them for latrines." I wouldn't lean against the walls, either."

"I'll bring a folding chair for you," I said, nudging the bucket the other way. I looked around at the chipped and stained walls, the grubby blanket folded on top of the mattress placed directly on the floor. "And a cot and a clean blanket to use as a mattress cover," I added, deciding to stand, like Clay.

He unwrapped a sandwich. I opened a Dr Pepper.

"Did you bring the chlorpheniramine and Cerumite for the cat?" he asked. "The warden's asked me twice already if you were coming."

I got the small bottle of pills and the mite medicine out of my pocket and handed them over. Clay put them carefully down on the cement by his feet.

"What about Lisa taking calls for me?"

I reassured him on that.

Only then did he take a bite of his sandwich. He was wearing one of the shirts I'd packed and fresh jeans. I could tell by the circles under his eyes that he hadn't slept. While he ate, I told him about Hugger and Monk.

"I'm glad you helped him out," Clay said. "I like Hugger. He's a knowledgeable stockman. You know what his real name is, don't you?"

"What?"

"Canfield."

"Canfield Baines. I can see why he prefers the nickname. How'd he get it?"

"Now that I don't know," Clay said, smiling genuinely for the first time since I'd arrived. "I'll have to ask him sometime. I bet it's a good story." He wiped his hands on the napkin. "You didn't happen to bring the Lysol and roach spray?"

"Clay, I'm so sorry. In the rush, I forgot."

"Don't worry about it," he said.

"How bad are the bugs?"

"I'm being crowded out," he said, smiling to let me know it really was okay. Except that I knew it wasn't. Clay is scrupulously clean and tidy, by nature as well as by the hygienic demands of his job. I hated it that, in the one thing he'd asked me to do for him, I'd let him down. I felt absurdly like crying.

"Tomorrow. I'll have them for you tomorrow when I bring your breakfast at ten," I said.

"I don't want you to have to bring me food. Or come every day, let alone twice a day, like these other poor women. It's too far and it'll take you away from the trading post too much."

"You have to eat and the prison doesn't feed you unless you pay, and even then—"

"The warden says there's a man around the corner who cooks for the men without families to do it for them. It's a bargain," Clay said, trying to make it into a joke. "Five dollars a day for two meals, delivered. I think that must be the gringo rate because one of the other prisoners tells me he pays three dollars."

"Probably beans and tortillas twice a day, every day. If you insist, let me make the arrangements." I didn't mention Claudia's cousin. I didn't want to remind him of Oscar's ordeal. Nor did I tell him that Radio Ojinaga had broadcast the fact of an arrest in the Mehendru murder case. If the bare announcement had nearly overwhelmed me by driving home

52

how much in jeopardy Clay was, how would he feel, locked up in this place?

A guard shouted, "Time's up."

It was one-ten. "I guess the visits are on border time," I said, grateful for the extra minutes.

Around us, women gathered up the baskets in which they'd brought food and clean laundry.

"You made the warden a happy man," Clay said, picking up the cat medicines from the cement floor and slipping them into his pocket. "Let me give you the rest of my good clothes to take home," he added, picking up the neatly folded trousers and shirt, his boots on top, and handing them to me.

"No doubt, in time, the cat will appreciate my effort, too," I said, keeping it light as he walked me toward the gate behind the other prisoners and their relatives.

"I'll see you tomorrow," I said firmly.

"Okay," he said. He squeezed my arm and I walked out the gate. Halfway to my pickup, I looked back and waved one more good-bye to the tall figure hanging on the gate.

TEN

Monday, April 15

The alarm sounded like a swarm of killer bees. Trying to shut it off, I knocked the digital clock to the floor. The plastic case cracked and the transparent front fell off, but the alarm buzzed on until I unplugged the damn thing.

A pale dawn hovered in the east as I brewed coffee and tried to shake the sluggishness from my mind. Was it only Monday? I felt as if I'd lived three lives since Friday night.

I had much to do in the hours before leaving for Ojinaga and my five-minute visit at ten o'clock with Clay. After breakfast, I devoted some time to Phobe and Jefe, taking them outside. I kept my back to the gusty wind while I picked up the pieces of the bird feeder the raccoons had destroyed. Phobe wandered slowly, head raised, sniffing the air for broadcast scents or putting her nose down into a small clump of fluff-grass that stank of possum. Jefe went at a trot, nose to the ground, sniffing madly in a seemingly erratic pattern that followed the path of a pocket mouse or a rat snake.

Forty minutes later, we were back inside. I opened the adjoining door to the big front room and Phobe and Jefe rushed in. The bobcat leaped from one displaytable to another while Jefe raced around the aisles, barking at her.

I telephoned Claudia to tell her I did want Oscar's wife to cook for Clay, at least until the end of the week. She'd anticipated me, in that she'd already discussed the possibility with Jesusita.

Claudia said, "Jesusita says Oscar will deliver the food in his cab. Just say when they should begin."

"I'm taking today's food," I told her.

"Then Jesusita will see to the rest of the week."

I wanted to pay more than just the cost of the groceries, but Claudia refused to allow it.

"The visits are five minutes—"

"At ten and two," Claudia said. "I remember. Take care, Texana. And try not to worry. I've started a novena."

I hoped that, in less time than the nine days of praying the rosary, Clay would be home.

I hung up and went to the storeroom for one of the folding chairs, then to the front. Phobe lay draped over the back of a display saddle and watched me with her round eyes. Jefe trotted along behind me as I took down one of two collapsible camp cots I had on sale, a large bottle of Lysol, Black Flag, a scrub brush, a box of assorted plastic utensils, a six-pack of canned grapefruit juice, and a tube of Carmex, the lip moisturizer Clay likes to carry in his vet's kit.

My stash complete, I opened the cot, placed a folded blanket on it, and shut it up again. I tied the chair and cot together with twine, the better to carry them, and put the other items in a plastic bag, tying it by the carry-loops to the handle of the chair.

That done, I went to the kitchen and opened the refrigerator, trying to decide what to cook for Clay. Getting out flour, baking powder, and a stick of butter, I made biscuits. While they browned in the oven, I fried the homemade sausage that one of my customers provides as partial payment of his grocery bill. When the sausages had cooled, I sliced the biscuits in half. Clay loved sausage-and-biscuit sandwiches. I made a dozen, wrapping them in foil.

At the last minute, after I had loaded everything into the pickup, I thought of one more item and went out to the clinic for a packet of flea killer for the warden's cat.

At eight-fifteen, as I was driving away from the trading post, I passed a patrol car driven by the deputy sheriff, Dennis Bustamante. We waved. Dennis usually stops at the trading post to have coffee and buy gas. If he needed a fill-up today, he knew Lucy Ramos, the postmistress in Polvo, kept my emergency key.

At El Cereso, I passed through the green gates once again, lugging the cot and chair. I had a fifty-peso note ready in my hand. The gatekeeper took it, I signed in, and he waved me by without so much as a glance at what I carried in the bag hanging from the chair. There were fewer visitors today, but I recognized many of the same women who'd been here on Sunday. The doorway into the offices was open and the warden's cat sat there, his long tail curled tightly around his front legs, watching me with baneful eyes. I could see damp, sticky patches in front of both ears, which meant Clay had dropped in the mite medicine. Zapata looked at me as if he knew I'd been part of the conspiracy to set thousands of minute bugs inside his ears scrambling as they suffocated.

My five minutes with Clay passed like five seconds and today there was no extra time before the guards shooed the visitors out.

I turned around and went home. A three-hour drive for a five-minute visit. Clay was right. I couldn't do this twice a day and run a business.

The telephone was ringing as I went in the back door. I grabbed the receiver, only to hear the disconnect. I hung up, took off my shoes, washed my hands at the sink, and then browsed in the refrigerator for my lunch. I found two chicken tenders in the freezer, heated them in the microwave, folded a slice of bread around each, and sat down within quick-pickup range of the telephone.

Thirty minutes later, Enrique Vera called back. "The hearing will be Thursday morning," he said. "The prosecutor is Alfonso Carmin, an assistant district attorney from Chihuahua. I'll meet with Señor Howard before the hearing and go over his evidence with him so we can be ready."

I felt as if I could breathe better. "Good. I'll tell Barton."

"Basically, what will happen is that the prosecutor will present the evidence collected so far," Enrique said. "I'll present your testimony and that of Señor Barton, then the magistrado will decide whether or not to hold Señor Jones as a suspect. I see no reason why he shouldn't be released, since he clearly was elsewhere the evening of the murder."

"That's good to hear," I said. "When you spoke with the prosecutor, did he explain why they arrested Clay in the first place?"

There was a pause, as if we'd lost the connection momentarily, then Enrique said, "I didn't speak with Señor Carmin. I talked to his assistant. He said he'd inform his boss that I'd called, but I'm guessing from his tone they're going to tell me nothing."

"What does that mean?"

"I don't know."

ELEVEN

For once I was glad that the trading post is too far out for garbage pickup. I compost kitchen waste. Once a month a family from across the river comes to pick up the bags I fill with washed bottles and cans, which they sell for reuse. Everything else we bury in a periodically bulldozed pit, except for newspapers, which we collect until there are enough to burn down by the river.

I was presently going through the stack of newspapers. The *Presidio International* is a weekly that runs to eight pages, max, for special events like the May Onion Festival, so I had months of back issues in the plastic storage bin behind the clinic. Phobe was helping me by trying to shred the newspapers before I could lift them out.

Mehendru had been murdered on a Saturday night in February. The first story about his murder had appeared on the following Thursday. I located that issue and lifted it out with all the ones on top of it and carried the bundle into the trading post. I got the paper scissors from my desk drawer, spread open each issue at the front counter, and clipped any story about the killing and the investigation. There were four in all.

The first was brief, giving only the salient facts, which I knew already. Around ten-thirty on February 23, preventivo Teo Lopez, investigating why a Silverado with Texas plates was in a no-parking zone in front of the La Iglesia de Nuestro Padre Jesús in Ojinaga, discovered a man slumped behind the wheel. Lopez tried unsuccessfully to rouse him, noticed blood on the seat and went around to the other side of the vehicle, finally determining that the man had been shot in the head. The dead man was identified as Zanjiv Mehendru by his driver's license, found in the wallet in his pocket.

Before I could read anymore, a woman came in to send a fax to her husband, who worked on a ranch near Fort Worth. I loaded the handwritten letter and sent it to the ranch-office fax number her husband had given her on his Easter trip home. She gave me a crumpled five-peso note as payment and I promised to get word to her if he responded. I'd bought the fax as soon as I opened the new trading post. It allowed my customers privacy of communication that the old pay telephone had not and it also kept our home and office numbers free.

I rang up the transaction and went back to my reading. There was little factual detail about the murder in the remainder of the clippings, except that the murder weapon was thought to be a small-caliber handgun, probably a .22-caliber. On March 8, the newspaper reported that the judiciales had been called in to investigate the death.

The story from the issue the week before Clay's arrest merely stated that the investigation by the judiciales had stalled after six weeks of vigorous efforts. There was one quote from the Chihuhua State Attorney General, Benito Vascón: "I have every confidence in the Assistant Attorney General José Cabello, whom I've appointed to head the murder investigation."

Zanjiv Mehendru had been a low-level bureaucrat, but

anything to do with border politics generated interest among the media on both sides. If the attorney general thought his office had a substantial case against Clay, why wouldn't Vascón himself want to head the investigation, cornering the media attention and the credit? Surely Clay was marginally safer because the case had passed down through several layers, until it landed on the desk of an assistant attorney general, Alfonso Carmin, the prosecutor.

Mehendru's obituary held some details about his life I hadn't known. He was fifty-one. He'd been born in Los Angeles. His father, Ravi, had been an engineer from Delhi, who had emigrated, become a naturalized American citizen and later had married an American named Jerrilyn Power. When Mehendru was seven years old, his father died. Two years later, his mother remarried and his stepfather, Aurelio Blancas, moved the family to Juárez. Exercising his right as an American citizen, Mehendru chose to attend high school in El Paso, where he eventually moved. After earning his Ph.D. in engineering from the University of Texas, he joined the faculty as a lecturer and consultant. In 1972, he married Patrice Tomms. He was appointed head of the U.S. section of the International Boundary and Water Commission in 1998.

The obituary included two quotes, one from Augusto Cigno, Mexico's Boundary and Water Commissioner in Juárez: "Dr. Mehendru was a man of vision and courage. I considered him a personal friend as well as a colleague. He will be missed."

The second was from United States Boundary and Water Commission spokesperson Paige Ward: "Commissioner Mehendru was a hands-on administrator respected by all who worked with him." Lukewarm, it seemed to me. Or polite. I wasn't the best judge, having met the man on only two occasions, both visits by Mehendru to the trading post after he'd bought his ranch upriver. On the second, he'd told me that he could get anything I carried more cheaply at the Wal-Mart in

El Paso. I didn't waste my breath trying to explain the overhead on a backcountry store versus a national chain.

A memorial service had been held at the Prado Funeral Home in El Paso, presumably because that is where the Boundary and Water Commission headquarters was and Mehendru's employees at the Commission wished to attend. Mehendru's remains had been cremated. Listed as survivors were Mehendru's son Daniel, age twenty-two; a half-sister, Kimberly Blancas de Garza of Chihuahua City; two half-brothers, Arturo Blancas of Chihuahua City, and Eduardo Blancas of Juárez; and his stepfather, Aurelio Blancas, of Juárez. No mention of a mother, so presumably she was dead. No mention of a wife or former wife, so Daniel's mother was dead, too. Poor Daniel.

Absent, too, was any reference to the Sloe Ranch, the two-thousand-acre property upriver that Mehendru had bought three years ago and where he spent weekends and holidays, well away from the office in El Paso.

I stapled the clippings together and slipped them into the top desk drawer. I'm a great believer in facts. I think if you put enough of them together, you can get answers. Mehendru's murder was odd, seemingly motiveless, and benefiting no one. That left the common-law wife.

TWELVE

Thursday, April 18

Vendors selling tacos, drinks, and prayer cards congregated on the sidewalk outside the drab municipal building adjacent to the prison, hawking their wares to those hungry for food or hope. By the door, two Tarahumara women sat in their voluminous skirts and head scarves, begging for coins.

Barton dropped a bill in the cardboard box one held up as we passed indoors. There was a wide hallway outside the courtrooms and we stopped there to wait for the hearing room to be unlocked.

Earlier, in the office at his house, Enrique had taken us over the testimony we would give in Clay's defense. It hadn't taken long, being straightforward and simple, a matter of stating time and place. I'd brought along Clay's appointment book for Enrique to copy in case it was needed in court, and Barton had the canceled check for Clay's veterinary services in his jacket pocket. Enrique was very pleased, very upbeat that Clay would be released. "There is no case," he said.

I caught sight of the Berreras among a group of people standing by the courtroom door just as it was unlocked from the inside. A middle-aged man in a black suit with a thin black necktie pushed the door back and held it open. Everyone went in except for a woman, very small, with dark hair and fine features, who stared at me. For a moment I thought she was going to cross the hall and speak to me, but she turned and went into the courtroom. Barton and I were nearly at the door when a man approached, hand outstretched.

"Mrs. Jones, we met two years ago . . . Eddie Salaman."

"Editor of *International*," I said, introducing Barton.

Salaman was a tall, bony fellow with big ears. He was wearing a short-sleeved shirt, no tie, brown pants, and boots.

"My colleague, Angel Girón," Salaman said, "editor of *La Voz de Ojinaga*."

Girón was dark and short, with thick curly hair, and round spectacles resting on a prominent nose. He wore khaki chinos with a blue knit crewneck, and tennis shoes that squeaked against the linoleum floor as the four of us walked into the courtroom. Salaman asked if he might call me at home for an interview, and when I agreed he moved away, taking a seat halfway near the front. Barton went to join the Berreras. Girón hung back, got a card out of his billfold, and handed it to me.

"My office address," he said. "If the magistrado decides to hold your husband, come and see me."

He went to join Salaman. I put the card in my pocket and walked to the front to join my friends.

The hearing room was small and slightly shabby, the desks and chairs more than a little battered. A flag of Mexico hung on the wall behind the magistrate's bench.

There were two men in front of the rail, one in shirtsleeves, who tidied papers on the magistrate's bench and paid no attention to those seating themselves. The other stood at one of the tables. He turned to watch, as if he found the small crowd entertaining. All his features, from his thick eyebrows to the tip of his prominent nose, to his mouth, had a slight downturn, as if gravity, rather than *gravitas,* gave essence to his character. He wasn't tall, but he gave the impression of height. Everything else about him looked silky and expensive—his light brown skin, his fine brown hair, his gray double-breasted suit, his red-and-yellow-striped tie, and his highly polished black shoes.

Enrique hurried past the rail and to the table directly in front of me. With his short black hair freshly cut and his blue suit he looked youthful but impressive, and very sure of himself.

He put his briefcase on the defense table and crossed to shake hands with the silky man. When he returned and took his seat, I leaned forward. "The man across the aisle, is he . . . ?

"Alfonso Carmin, the assistant D.A. who's prosecuting."

As I leaned back, Barton said quietly, "Mario says there are reporters here from *La Jornada, Reforma,* and *El Universal.*"

Multiple heavy footsteps rang on the hard linoleum floor of the aisle and I twisted around in my seat to see. Clay, wearing the suit I'd dropped off at the prison early that morning and escorted by two guards, walked by, shooting me a fast fading smile. One guard indicated the chair next to Enrique and Clay sat down. Enrique murmured something to him and shook his hand.

"Magistrado Emilio Resendez," announced the man in shirtsleeves.

A door at the front opened and a close-bearded man in black robes entered and took his seat at the bench. He peered at us myopically, nodding first at Alfonso Carmin, then in the general direction of Enrique.

Clay sat perfectly still, his back ramrod-straight in the hard chair.

Alfonso Carmin removed an impressive stack of papers

from his briefcase, rose to his feet, and addressed the court in a voice as smooth as his looks. "Magistrado, the state will present irrefutable evidence against Clay Jones, a nortéamericano, in the murder of Zanjiv Mehendru, also a nortéamerico, in Ojinaga on Saturday, the twenty-third of February. The coroner's report confirms the date of death and the manner, a small-caliber gunshot wound to the head at close range." Carmin handed a document to the man in shirtsleeves, who presented it to the magistrate. Resendez gave it a glance and put it aside.

Carmin looked around at the courtroom, as if to gather his audience, and said, "We have an eyewitness to the murder whom we now call, Aida Machuca."

Enrique looked at Clay, who shook his head in total puzzlement.

Entering the courtroom through the same door the magistrate had used came an anorexically thin woman. She wore a white scoop-necked blouse intended for the bosom that might have been, a short black skirt that rustled like taffeta as she walked to the witness stand, and high-heeled red shoes. Her black hair had streaked orange highlights and hung about her shoulders in a tangled mass. Pinkish scars dotted her brown arms. She sat nervously on the edge of the gray metal folding chair to the magistrate's left and directly in front of Carmin.

Carmin said, "Your name is Aida Machuca?"

"Yes," she said, her eyes locked on him as if he were a rattlesnake coiled to strike.

"You're a prostitute, are you not?"

"Yes."

"And in that profession you were at the plaza near La Iglesia de Nuestro Padre Jesús, on the night of the twenty-third of February, a Saturday."

"Yes."

"You were there at ten?"

"Yes."

"It was about five minutes after ten that you saw a white Silverado pickup drive up and park in front of the church."

"Yes."

"Could you see the driver?"

"Yes. It was a man."

"Where were you standing?"

"Under the portico of the presidencia."

"And from there, you saw something else."

"A man came up to the driver of the pickup. He pulled something out of his pocket. He leaned over close to the window. There was a shot and the man ran away."

"The man who ran, where did he go?"

"Around the corner of the church," Machuca said.

"Describe the man you saw approach the driver's side, fire a shot, and run away," Carmin instructed her.

"He was very tall, with short light hair. He had on jeans and a dark jacket."

"There was something else about him, wasn't there?" Carmin prompted.

"Yes. He was a gringo."

And when the judiciales questioned you, you admitted you'd witnessed the murder and described the man you saw."

"Yes."

"Is he in court today?" Carmin said.

"Yes. He's there," she said, pointing toward Clay.

"That's all," Carmin said, sitting down.

Resendez looked over at Enrique, who rose to his feet. "Have you questions for the witness?

"Yes, Magistrado," he said, turning to the witness. "There's a streetlight at the corner by the church. Was it on that night?"

"That light's been broken for months," Machuca said, then bit her lip as Carmin jumped up.

"The judiciales have checked," he said. "That light on the far end of the plaza works and is sufficient to provide enough light to see."

"Señorita Machuca, are you a drug addict?" Enrique asked.

"I don't see the relevance," Carmin said firmly.

"Nor do I," Resendez said. "Take the witness out."

Aida Machuca jumped to her feet.

The man in the shirtsleeves escorted her through the same door by which she had entered.

"Licenciado Vera," Resendez said, "have you evidence to present?"

"I have two witnesses present who place Señor Jones over fifty miles from Ojinaga at the time of the murder."

Resendez looked over at Carmin.

"I expect additional evidence against the suspect as the investigation continues, Magistrado," Carmin said.

"The prisoner will remain in custody," Resendez said, already on his feet. Simultaneously, the guards were at Clay's sides, taking him out.

Carmin stuffed the stack of papers into his briefcase, snapped it closed, and headed toward the door. The reporters were so taken by surprise they hadn't moved. Enrique grabbed his briefcase and started down the aisle after Carmin. I followed, Barton and the Berreras with me.

In the hallway, Enrique, swollen with anger, stood in front of Carmin, who was saying calmly, "You have nothing to complain about. Your client's getting due process."

"You sandbagged us!" Enrique shouted.

Mario put his hand on his godson's arm.

Carmin gave Enrique a long look, then he said carefully and in a low voice, "Don't be foolish. You know how things work." He looked up, caught my eyes locked on his face, and turned away. The swarm of reporters who'd just come out of the court ran to catch up.

Enrique moved as if to follow, but Mario drew him back. "Come, let's find someplace where we can talk quietly."

Enrique looked at me, then let his godfather lead him

away. Olivia put her arm through mine, saying, "Come, we'll sort this out."

I registered her words, but my mind was on the pity I had seen in Alfonso Carmin's eyes when they met mine.

THIRTEEN

Come to my office at the bakery," Olivia suggested, as we stood on the hot pavement. She looked at me for approval.

"I'll meet you there," I told her. She and Mario left with Enrique in tow.

"Is there anything I can do?" Barton asked.

I thanked him and told him he might as well go home. I watched as he walked to his Yukon, got in, and drove away, leaving me feeling inexplicably lonely. I went to my Ford, not bothering with the air conditioner for the short drive to the bakery.

There was a parking space in front. The doors were open and tantalizing smells of cinnamon and anise hung in the air. I bought a copy of today's *La Voz de Ojinaga* from the vendor on the corner. Clay's name jumped out at me from the headline. He was so private. If he knew, he would hate the publicity almost as much as he hated being arrested. I put the newspaper in the pickup and went into the bakery.

Behind a wooden counter stacked with bolillos, empanadas, and pan dulce, two young women filled brown paper sacks for customers, ringing up the charges on a massive brass cash register. The employees knew me and thought nothing of it as I went past the counter and into the furnace-like atmosphere of the baking room, with its deeply arched brick walls, black with smoke from the wood fires that heated the brick ovens lining one wall. Two young men and one woman, glistening with sweat, shaped dough into loaves and placed them on wide wooden paddles used to slide them onto the oven racks.

Olivia's office was down a hallway past the baking room and well enough insulated by thick adobe so that one did not feel the radiant heat so much. A ceiling fan whirling high overhead helped.

The Berreras and Enrique Vera, a folded newspaper in front of him, sat at one end of a long table. The opposite end was cluttered with invoice pads, a sheaf of bills under a paperweight of the rain god Tlatoc, bundles of brown paper sacks, and other items necessary to Olivia's business. As I came in, she rose to pour coffee from the urn on the sideboard, handing round the cups and a plate of turnovers. I took one to be polite. I was too upset about what had happened in court to have an appetite, despite the fact that I hadn't eaten breakfast.

Enrique, too, was consumed by the morning's disaster.

"The hearing was a joke," he said, his voice raspy with anger. "What a witness! Did you see the needle scars on her arms? Keep her supplied so she can shoot up and she'd have said El Presidente shot Mehendru if Carmin told her to. The only time the truth passed her lips was when she said the streetlight was out. Carmin is so arrogant he doesn't care if his witness is caught in a lie."

"This is the kind of justice mexicanos face every day," Olivia said angrily. "Vicente Fox promised us he'd clean up the corruption. Ha!"

"That will take decades of work," Mario said reasonably,

"and he has no power to touch state politicos and judiciales."

"Is that what Alfonso Carmin meant about how things work?" I asked.

"Carmin is being pressured by someone who can destroy his career if he doesn't go along," Enrique said.

"The attorney general?" I asked.

"That's my guess," Enrique said. "That would explain why no one would talk to me. Even the usual whispers one hears when pressure is being applied have vanished. Did you notice the magistrado? He was so nervous, he was sweating. Clearly he knew Señor Jones was to be held, no matter how obviously contrived the evidence."

"Are you sure of this?" I asked, getting truly scared and scrambling for some hope that he might be wrong.

"As sure as I can be," Enrique said.

"Why Clay?"

"That I don't know," Enrique said.

"We've been talking about who can best help you," Mario said.

"You need someone with pull," Enrique said.

"Someone who's a member of Chihuahua's camarilla, you know the word?" Mario said.

I nodded. "A power clique. You have someone in mind?" I said.

"This man," Enrique said, sliding across a copy of *El Diario de Chihuahua* and putting a finger on the front-page photograph of a middle-aged man with thick gray hair and eyes as soulful as a basset hound's. *Tito Berg: La Hormiga Atómica*, the caption read.

"Why do they call him the atomic ant?"

"Because he's everywhere, on all the big cases," Mario said. "Even the attorney general will have to return Berg's telephone calls."

"He knows the right people," Enrique said.

"And plenty of wrong ones," Olivia said harshly, a pained expression on her face.

71

"You don't agree with this?" I said.

She made a dismissive gesture. "I don't like the people he represents. Drug dealers, kidnappers, politicians."

"Those are the people who need lawyers," Mario said.

"You think Clay needs him?" I asked.

"If he can free guilty clients," Mario said, "surely he can do the same for an innocent man."

"As much as I hate to agree, Mario is right," Olivia said.

Olivia's words settled it. No one hated dishonesty and political corruption more than she.

"Berg lives in Chihuahua City?" I asked.

Enrique nodded. "I'll telephone him, if you like, on your behalf and explain what Señor Jones is up against."

"Please do," I told him.

FOURTEEN

As we left the bakery, Enrique asked if I planned to stay and see Clay.

"Yes." I checked my watch. Twelve-forty. A little over an hour until the permitted five-minute visit at two o'clock.

"Tell him I'm sorry," Enrique said. "I did my best."

"I know you did."

We parted at the curb. I unlocked the pickup, got in, opened *La Voz de Ojinaga* and made myself read the front-page story about Clay's arrest. Beyond identifying him, the article mostly rehashed the little that was known about the Mehendru murder. At the end of the last paragraph, credit for information used in compiling the story was given to Mercedes Solar.

Was Zanjiv Mehendru's common-law wife covering the murder case and trial? Had she been in court today?

I dropped the newspaper behind the seat, opened the glove compartment, and moved the owner's manual to take out a pen and a small spiral notebook. I locked the pickup and walked to the east side of the plaza to the presidencia.

Inside the cavernous, windowless lobby, the temperature was ten degrees cooler, thanks to thick adobe walls. Today I didn't stop, as I usually do when I'm in this extraordinary building, to stare upward at the huge flat figures of Diego Rivera–style murals, which cover the top half of the deeply arched walls.

Instead, I passed along a branching hall, looking for the municipal tax office, hoping they might give me Mercedes Solar's address. I found the right door, identified by title on the cloudy glass insert, turned the blackened brass knob, and walked in. Behind a high counter, a young woman sat on a stool.

I explained whom I was trying to locate and asked if she might be on the tax rolls.

"That might take a long time to check."

I knew it was a long shot, but I asked for the telephone directory. She slid off the stool and disappeared into the next room, returning after several minutes with a thin directory so old that the pages had curled. There was no date on it, but I guessed it probably dated back at least five years. A number of pages had been ripped out. Some of the listings were alphabetized, but many were random, reflecting a home where someone had moved in, taking over the previous tenant's five-digit number. Newer numbers had been added with no thought of any order at all.

"No luck?" the clerk said, as I handed the directory back.

"No luck, but thanks for your help."

She looked back over her shoulder toward some partitioned cubicles. "Rosa, do you know a Mercedes Solar?"

"I know her books."

"She's a writer?" I said to the invisible Rosa.

Rosa emerged from her cubicle with a soft-cover book that she handed to me. The cover art was a color-washed line drawing depicting a small adobe house, and beyond, a man plowing a field with mules. Across the top of the cover, the title, *En Tierra de Nod,* was lettered in gold against bright red; at the bottom was the author's name, Mercedes Solar. I turned the book over. There was no photograph of the author, but there was a brief biography.

> Fiction writer and political activist Mercedes Solar was born in Juárez. After attending the National Autonomous University in Mexico City, she returned to Juárez to live, while teaching Spanish at a junior college in El Paso. She was one of the founding members of Taller Literario de Juárez. The author lives in Ojinaga.

I noted the name and address of the publisher, Visión Books on 110 Calle Madero, Ojinaga, and handed the book back to Rosa, thanking her for her help.

I found the modest publishing office just a few blocks away at the corner opposite the furniture store.

An intelligent-looking, genial man seated at a rolltop desk piled with papers greeted me as I came in. Justo Aranda explained to me that he was sole proprietor, editor, and publisher of Visión Books. I bought a copy of *En Tierra de Nod* and pretended to read the biographical information anew.

"Does Ms. Solar hold a writers' workshop here in Ojinaga?" I asked.

"She does," Aranda said. "Are you interested?"

"Very much," I said, lying unashamedly in Clay's behalf. "Could you give me her telephone number?"

"Mercedes has been on the TelMex waiting list for two years and still no telephone. Try her house on Calle Lerdo, the first street past the open-air market. It's white. You can't miss it."

Outside, I jotted down her street in the notebook and checked the time. A little past one. Too far to go to Solar's house. I slid the notebook into my pocket and felt the edge of the card Angel Girón had given me. I'd forgottten about him.

What had he said? If they hold your husband, come see me. His business address was a street near the prison. I drove straight there.

The newspaper editor had piles of past issues of *La Voz de Ojinaga* on sale at the front counter of the warehouselike print shop, with its old presses and an equally old pressman working on some car-rally posters.

"The printing business supports the newspaper," he told me. "Our readers are loyal, but businesses are afraid to advertise with me. Too iconoclastic. They're afraid the political jefes and the narcotraficantes will take notice."

"And do they? Take notice?"

He gave an expressive lift of his shoulders. "I've had a little trouble, but someone's got to tell the truth. That's why I wanted to talk to you. Let me show you what I have."

He walked back to his desk, opened the middle drawer, pulled out some papers, and handed them to me.

There were three pages stapled together, each more or less the same, lined double columns with handwritten—in more than one hand—names and times.

"What am I looking at?" I asked.

"Photocopies of the jail intake sheet for the twenty-second, the twenty-third, and the twenty-fourth of February." Girón pointed to a name in the second column of the first page, the sheet for Friday. "Aida Machuca. Her street name is La Panocha. She was jailed at eight P.M. Now turn over to the third page. See the date—Sunday, the twenty-fourth? Now look halfway down the second column. She was released at eight that night. They held her in jail for forty-eight hours. The prosecutor's eyewitness was in jail when the murder was committed."

Here was proof of everything Enrique believed true. Clay was being deliberately framed by someone. "How did you get these?"

"The police chief gave them to me," Girón said. "More important, last Tuesday the chief personally took copies and presented them to Magistrado Resendez."

"So Resendez knew the prosecutor's witness was lying," I said, feeling a surge of anger so intense I felt flushed. "Why did the police chief—"

"He's Santo Girón. My brother doesn't like injustices any better than I do," Angel Girón said. "You can keep those. I made copies for myself. My column this week makes this information public, but I thought you should see the proof for yourself."

"When did your brother give these to you?"

"Right after Resendez told him to mind his own business."

FIFTEEN

The wind had picked up fiercely, whirling dust in the air. I waited in the pickup until the gatekeeper emerged from his shed and rolled back the heavy green gates of El Cereso.

As I crossed the street, a decade-old Chevrolet Celebrity pulled up and a potbellied, bowlegged man in black pants and a Dallas Cowboys T-shirt got out carrying a dish covered with a clean white cloth.

"Oscar," I called.

He turned, looking momentarily puzzled, then smiled broadly. "Señora Jones!"

"It's been a few years, Oscar," I said, catching up with him. "I see you have a new car. I like it." The "new" was relative, his previous vehicle having been a '78 Pontiac.

"It's a good little car. With the hatchback, I make a little extra money hauling things for people."

"I want to thank you and Jesusita for helping us out with the meals."

"We will help as long as you need us." He added sorrowfully, "It's all over town about the magistrado's decision."

The gatekeeper motioned us to hurry. Oscar accompanied me to Clay's cell and exchanged the fresh meal of chicken tacos for the morning's dirty plate, then left.

Clay told me to sit on the folding chair. He put the plate on a plastic crate and sat on the blanket-covered cot I'd brought. The cell was stifling. The outside temperature was in the high nineties and the windowless cell was at least that hot; besides, no wind penetrated here. Clay had taken off the suit he'd worn to court. It lay neatly folded beside him on the blanket. He looked exhausted, his face gray and waxen.

"I didn't expect today," he said, confusion in his voice. "It was over before I could take in what happened."

I took the jail intake forms out of my pocket and handed them to him. "It seems you have unexpected friends." I didn't mention the unexpected enemies. Clay would realize that as soon as he saw the sheets.

After I explained the documents and the source, Clay said, "Does it help or hurt to know I'm being framed?"

"It helps—"

"This Aida Machuca, she didn't decide to lie on her own. Who's behind it—the prosecutor?"

The guard called time. Our five minutes was up.

"Things may move slowly," I said, "but you're going to get out."

We got to our feet. Clay kissed me on my forehead. "I'd better give you my suit and my dirty clothes for the laundry," he said. He handed me the bundle.

By the time I'd crossed the street, I'd made up my mind to see Mercedes Solar. In order to find out who was framing Clay, I had to know who had killed Zanjiv Mehendru and why. I had to start somewhere. Solar likely knew him better than anyone.

I had difficulty finding the right street among the four that, depending on the direction from which one came, could be as the publisher had described it: ". . . the first street past the open-air market." The fact that Ojinaga has few street signs didn't help. I cruised by the market for the second time, eyeing the tables piled with cheap trinkets and toys, vegetables wilting in the sun, hanging nopal cactus pads, strings of dried chiles, and stacks of tortillas.

The street might have been difficult to find, but in a town that is covered in dust, the house shone in the light like a white beacon.

I found a parking space farther along the street and walked back to the pair of antique wooden doors in the high adobe wall that enclosed the lot adjacent to the house. Somewhere behind it, water ran with great force. I pulled the chain tied to the handle of a brass bell that rang with an atonal sound.

An exasperated voice from within muttered something I couldn't distinguish, then one door swung inward and a woman with a water hose in her hand stood there. She stared at me for an instant, then dropped the hose, stepped back, and said, "Please, come in, Señora Jones."

"I recognize you from court, too," I said, stepping inside. She was the woman who had stood by the door before the hearing began who'd looked as if she was going to speak to me. She had changed from the suit she'd worn in court to a loose white blouse over slim-fitting black pants.

"Excuse me while I turn the water off," she said. "I have to hose down the walls once or twice a week this time of year or they'd be the color of dirt all the time."

She moved with grace, a middle-aged woman so small of stature she appeared almost fragile. Her thick black hair was parted in the middle and cut to neckline length.

The garden had a fountain beneath a desert willow, the surface of its water flecked with spent blooms. There were chairs and a table, potted palms, and a bright red bougainvillea.

"Have you had lunch?" Mercedes Solar asked.

"Please don't trouble—"

"Come inside," she said, walking off across the small patio toward a door of the house.

I followed her into a long rectangular room with the adobe brick exposed on the walls. The furnishings were plain and few. A curtain across the far end divided the room from the rest of the quarters. One wall held bookcases, another a series of cork sheets pinned with photos, messages, quotations, clippings, cartoons. There was a long table, surrounded with chairs of varying style, with stacks of papers weighted down with river stones, more books, a cup with pens, a typewriter, and a CD player.

Mercedes Solar said, "I have whiskey, tequila, and gin."

"Whiskey, please," I said, "straight up."

"Yes, it's been that kind of day, hasn't it," she said, pouring us both a generous glass. "Sit down. I'm going to prepare us some food and then we'll talk." She put on a CD, something New Age and soothing, before stepping behind the curtain. I heard a gentle clatter of cutlery and dishes.

I'd finished the whiskey by the time she returned with a loaded tray and set two places at the table. "This is chicken salad with jalapeños and zucchini," she said. "The dressing is vinegar, jalapeño sauce, and tomato purée."

We ate without conversation. The whiskey had eased my tension, reducing to a manageable eccentricity the oddity of my sitting down to a meal with the common-law wife of the man my husband was accused of murdering.

While I mopped the bowl with my last flour tortilla, she refilled our glasses, half whiskey, half water this time. "As you're driving," she said.

"You're being more than kind," I said. "Why, under the circumstances? I half expected you to close the door in my face."

"Because you're doing exactly what I'd do," she said. "I, too, want to know the truth and I think we both know it's not going to come out in court. I saw Angel Girón talking with you before the hearing. I assumed he was telling you about the proof he has that the witness is lying. Someone wants your husband to pay for what someone else did and you and I both want to know who that person is."

I took her words at face value because of the sense of outrage her tone and manner conveyed. If it were an act, if I was being fooled by someone with an agenda other than the truth, I was too tired to perceive it. The stress of the past week had hit me in a wave of fatigue. I'd have given much just to crawl into a bed and sleep for hours, but I badly wanted to understand Solar's relationship with Mehendru. She seemed to feel the stress, too, and got up to get the bottle of whiskey. I covered my glass with my hand. "I think I need coffee," I said regretfully.

She vanished beyond the curtain again, returning with two mugs of hot coffee just as I was nodding off. As we sipped, I eyed a bas-relief plaque about twelve inches long that lay in the center of the table.

"Don Quixote and Sancho," she said. "It's a copy of the original from the Plaza Cervantine in Juárez. Zanjiv gave it to me."

"You grew up in Juárez," I said, recalling the book-cover biography and judging by her hands and the subtle lines around her eyes and mouth that she had to be near Mehendru's age. "So did he. Did you know him as a boy?"

"He and my brother were best friends. I was five years younger. I adored them both." She touched one hand to the plaque. "My father was a customs broker, arranging export to the other side for all sorts of goods. We lived in a house on the Plaza Cervantine. But it wasn't for memory that Zanjiv gave me this," she said. "He liked it because it reminded him of us, our relationship. He said I was Don Quixote and he was my Sancho. In many ways, he was right."

"What giants are you trying to cut down?" I asked.

She straightened slightly in her chair and smiled, not at me, but at herself. "I was very young when I decided that I was going to be a novelist," she said. "In those days, I thought of writing as a way to help people understand each other, to elevate sensibilities, to educate."

"That's no bad motive," I said.

"Zanjiv said I'd merely chosen the lesser of two evils, try-

ing to explain people instead of trying to change them, like a
social worker or psychologist. Zanjiv believed that people
were what they were, that no one could change them. But
then, Zanjiv was a man of principle. He seldom let people get
in the way."

"Was that what got him killed?" I said.

"It may well have," she said sadly. "I loved Zanjiv, but I
know he wasn't a man who endeared himself to others."

If the two of you were so very different—"

She laughed lightly. "We shared childhood and adoles-
cence. We both lost those dearest to us when we were young.
Zanjiv his father, I, a brother and father. We were both lonely.
At first, I loved him because he loved me, but later . . ." She
glanced around the pleasant room as if seeing it through her
dead lover's eyes. "He liked to come here and forget everything else. Here, together, we were young again."

Her frankness made me bold. "Why didn't you marry?" I
said.

She neither checked my curiosity nor allowed it to embar-
rass her.

"The only reason I see for marriage is to raise children,"
she said. "We were past all that."

In her answer, I saw why Mehendru found her appealing.
She made it clear what one might expect from her. No one
could feel taken in by such a person.

"Then why the common-law marriage document?" I
asked.

"Zanjiv rarely insisted with me, knowing it would do no
good. But on that one thing, he did." She paused. "It was so
unlike him that I knew it must be very important to him. So I
went along with it."

I wanted to ask her about Aida Machuca, but it was over
the top to ask even a frank woman if her lover was on familiar terms with a whore. Before the effects of the whiskey
washed caution out of my brain and indiscretion onto my
tongue, I got to my feet.

"Thank you for talking with me," I said.

"You're welcome," she said, rising also, "but it wasn't disinterested courtesy. I want you to do something for me."

"If I can."

We were walking toward the patio, to the garden entrance. Perhaps having second thoughts, she didn't speak again until she pushed open the wooden door to let me out.

"Do you know Zanjiv's son, Daniel?" she asked tentatively.

"He used to come into my trading post occasionally."

She nodded once, as if confirming something to herself, then said, "I've never met him. What kind of person is he?"

"He's polite, intelligent, well-mannered."

"Would you bring him to see me?"

"What makes you think he'll even talk to me, now?"

"For the same reason that I talked with you. Because I don't think anyone believes the right person has been arrested for Zanjiv's murder." She paused, blinking away a film of tears. "Zanjiv was here that night, you know."

"The night he was killed?"

"He always spent Saturdays with me. I cooked for us. He left at nine-thirty, as usual."

"He had a long drive home," I said, thinking of the hours it would surely take to get from here to his ranch, though we locals are inured to long miles. "Was he parked here, in front of your house?"

"Yes," she nodded. "I wondered about that, too. Why the Silverado was found in front of the church. I'm a mile or more from the square."

"Maybe he wanted to go inside the church?"

"Zanjiv was not religious. He relied on himself. He considered that sufficient."

"Then maybe whoever coached Aida Machuca told her part of the truth," I said. "Maybe he went there to meet the person who killed him."

"And not be able to get back home?" she said. "The bridge closes at ten."

"Would he have come back here to stay?"

"No. He never spent the night. I go to bed early and get up early to write. He knew that. He wouldn't have disturbed me."

"When did you learn that . . . he'd been killed?"

"Angel Girón came to tell me after he learned of it from his brother." She paused. "There's something else. After Zanjiv left me, maybe five or six minutes later, I heard a gunshot. These adobe walls are thick. The shot sounded dull. It could have come from right out here or from down the block, but I'm sure it was a shot. I didn't think much about it at the time. Around here, people fire off guns when they've had too much to drink, or to celebrate something, or to scare off stray dogs."

We left it at that, neither of us putting into words that she might have heard the shot that killed Mehendru, his killer driving the Silverado to the square afterward.

I promised her I'd let Daniel know she wanted to see him and started for home. My instinct said I could trust Solar, but it was Clay's freedom I would be placing in jeopardy if I trusted wrongly.

SIXTEEN

At home, I found a note from Claudia tucked between the screen and the inside door.

Texana, come to Casa Azul for dinner. A few friends will be coming by to show support.

I wasn't hungry and I was tired, but I couldn't say no to Claudia after she'd gone to so much trouble to help me. I dropped my keys on the counter, went to the blinking answering machine and played back the tape: *Texana, it's Lisa, call me when convenient; T.R. here, I got thirty calves that need vaccinating when Clay's available.*

I put off returning Lisa's call until tomorrow. The rancher would hear soon enough about Clay being held. We may be miles from each other, but gossip travels at light speed.

I fed Phobe and Jefe, changed into jeans and a T-shirt, poured a glass of milk, and telephoned my father to let him know what had happened.

"If you need money," he said, "there's always the ranch. I

hear land values around here have gone up lately. I expect it would sell fast."

I thanked him, knowing that I would never take him up on the offer. That place was his safe haven, the quiet and isolation the only things that made his depression managable.

After the conversation with my father, I put all thoughts on hold and cleaned the oven. At six-forty, I tidied myself up and drove to Claudia's.

The community of Polvo revolves around the small white adobe church, with its adjacent walled cemetery. The one-room school closed two years ago. Beyond it, facing the river, is the Ramoses' home and post office, with big cottonwood trees out front that Lucy planted when she was a bride. As I drove past the double line of flat-roofed adobes and the scattering of trailer homes that make up the rest of the community, the town mutts came out to trail my pickup.

Polvo had been founded by a handful of families, my father's among them. Franco Ricciotti, his grandfather, had left northern Italy in 1885, part of a group of growers and winemakers welcomed in Chihuahua by the government of Porfirio Díaz. The raids deep into Mexico by the Apache and Comanche for slaves, mules, and cattle sent the growers into Texas, most settling near Del Rio, where the San Felipe Springs provided water. The memory of his first sight of the Trans-Pecos region stayed with my great-grandfather Franco, and in 1888 he returned, renting a room in Marfa while he scouted out a place to settle. Within a few months, he paid the state of Texas a dollar for a section of land and hired workers from Ojinaga to build a trading post on the wagon road running along the slight rise above the floodplain of the Rio Grande. The only nearby people were three families—the Lunas, the Risas, and Ybarras, living on scattered small holdings. The trading post drew them closer in. Not only them. Others, like the Howards and the Masterses, came to settle in the then-lush river valley, where they grew cotton in the silt-rich soil of the floodplain.

Every memory of my life was bound up in this place, these people. Their history was my history, inseparable. What a comfort to live among those who understand without being told, who see with our eyes, who feel with our hearts. How could I doubt Mercedes Solar and Zanjiv Mehendru had been drawn together because of a shared past.

I turned onto the short road that ended at the Reyeses' vivid blue adobe and found it lined with pickups and old cars. Ruben Reyes, Claudia's husband, must have been watching out the window for me. His thin short figure was on the threshold shouting a welcome before I'd slammed shut the pickup door.

"She's here," he sang out over his shoulder at the same time he grasped my hand to pull me inside. The tiny restaurant was packed. People shouted my name, shook my hand. Someone put a bottle of Modelo beer in my hand, another pulled out a chair. Claudia rushed from the kitchen to kiss my cheek.

I set the beer down on the nearest table and looked around at the Lunas, the Risas; our oldest resident, Eva Ybarra; the Pachecos; our local drunk, John Henry Curzon; all of the Ramos family, among others.

"We drew up a petition and all one hundred and twenty-five of us signed," Claudia said, handing me a clipboard.

FREE CLAY JONES was printed at the top of each page, and beneath was one sentence: We respectfully petition the Attorney General of Chihuahua to intervene on behalf of Clay Jones, an innocent man, and order Magistrate Emilio Resendez to release him from El Cereso.

I put the clipboard on the table. "How did you find out about the outcome of the hearing so fast?" I said.

"Dennis Bustamante heard about it in Presidio. He told Jerry Ayrs and Jerry told me when he delivered a package. I called Lucy and told her to let everyone know and, as you can see, she did."

Jerry Ayrs is a rancher who makes ends meet by working as a UPS driver out of Marfa. His long route covers most of the county. We depend on him to bring not only packages, but news.

The door opened and in came a bearlike man, his red beard streaked with white, dressed very much as he'd been seven years ago, when I first met him, in a black shirt, jeans, and sandals.

"Am I late?" Jack Raff said in his sonorous baritone.

Our once-resident priest, who'd been briefly exiled to Chicago, had officially retired and returned to live among us once again. He came straight to me, took both my hands in his, and said, "No need to tell me Clay is innocent. I know that. The only thing surer is that we'll not give up or give in until he's home again."

Everyone clapped.

"Now, I hear there's a petition going," he said, releasing my hands. "Where do I sign?" I pointed out the clipboard. He reached for a pen clipped to his shirt pocket, leaned over, and signed his name large and bold, like his personality. Straightening, he smiled at the room in general.

"I'd like to have prayers for Clay's freedom being said every hour of the day," he said. "Saint Raymond is in a good position to help us, as he's face-to-face with God. He's the patron of the falsely imprisoned. We'll ask him to petition God directly on Clay's behalf. I'll be in the church this very night, should any of you wish to join me."

Eva Ybarra and Annie Luna came over to say they'd each take an hour. The priest got out his pen and the three sat down together. I heard the tops popping on more Modelo beer bottles. Polvo can make a party out of most occasions. Claudia had put salsa and chips on the tables and people milled about, eating and talking. She came over and asked me to come into the kitchen and have a real meal, but I told her that I'd had lunch too late to be hungry.

"I'll wrap something for you to take home," she said, "so you can have it tomorrow."

Jack made his way back to me and sat down at the table.

"I thought of visiting Clay tomorrow," he said.

"He'd like that," I said. I explained the schedule for visits.

"I'll go then," Jack said. "Five minutes tomorrow. On Sunday, if you don't mind company, I'll play uncle."

I nodded, more grateful than I could say. Over the years, I'd met a lot of priests, many of them mediocre, a few venal. Jack Raff is one of those virile, vital men who'd chosen God and the Church for all the right reasons and stayed with it because vows meant something to him.

"These people are one hundred percent on Clay's side, you know," he said, sensing my need for comfort.

"Is there really a Saint Raymond, or did you make him up?" I asked, sniffing back tears.

"The blessed saint is as real as I am, only much more courageous and holy. He was a Spaniard who died in the thirteenth century. He devoted his life to ransoming captives from the Moors. When his money ran out, he gave himself up to them so that a few more prisoners might go free."

"We may need him," I said.

"We'll fund-raise, too," Jack said. "This is going to cost you more than just sleepless nights. I know you must be exhausted, but before you go I want you to tell these good people about the hearing, your impressions. It's important they know facts, not just the newspaper version of them."

"All right."

He called everyone to attention and I got to my feet and gave them a summary of the hearing, including the eyewitness who'd been locked in jail at the crucial time.

My friends were as stunned by my blunt account as I'd been by the actual event. Their bravado vanished, replaced by somber concern that the situation might be beyond being easily righted by petitions to man or God.

SEVENTEEN

Friday, April 19

One thing about owning a trading post, if you need to talk to someone, sooner or later that person is bound to show up.

My business always picks up toward the weekends, when people want videos, beer, and snack food. On this Friday, I was busier than usual with customers from both sides of the river coming in to buy and to commiserate with me over Clay's imprisonment.

Of necessity, I carry a wide range of things folks out here in the backcountry may need, sometimes only one or two of an item, like a well-pressure gauge. Such things may gather dust for months, then suddenly sell. Ever since we moved into the new building, I've had a three-tier saddle rack, bought in a burst of entrepreneurial enthusiasm, taking up more space than it should. The first customer of the day bought it.

Over the next two hours, I rang up sales for two galvanized garbage cans, a pair of wire cutters, one tape measure, iodine wound spray, dehorning paste, Absorbine horse liniment, three twenty-pound bags of Science Diet Canine Growth, and two bags of numbered ear tags for cattle. All that in addition to the usual canned goods and my best sellers, after deep-fried pork skins, masa harina, sugar, coffee, and dried beans. One woman bought an entire box of Grisi brand Jabon Leche de Burra, donkey's milk soap, that normally sells one bar at a time. It seemed much of the community had realized that cash was going to be needed to fight Clay's legal battles and they were trying mightily to help me.

There were five or six more people roaming the aisles when Daniel Mehendru's friend Crosse Hickman walked in. I'd told Mercedes Solar that I'd let Daniel know she wanted to see him, but I had no intention of doing so directly. Crosse would be the perfect go-between.

Daniel was two years younger than Crosse and less mature, making for an uneven, perhaps unlikely, friendship. But in our region, where most young people with ambition have to leave to find work, friendship is as much an exercise of availability as of choice. And Crosse, amiable and easygoing, liked people.

He ambled toward the small Roper refrigerator where I chill the canned drinks, a tall, lanky young man in faded jeans, well-worn boots, and a T-shirt from an Austin City Limits concert featuring Tres Hermanos. He got a can of A&W Rootbeer and popped the top.

I watched him walk the aisles, greeting people and chatting, completely self-assured. In our only prolonged conversation, when he'd first arrived in the region two years ago, he'd told me that he'd just graduated from Texas Tech with a business degree and he was ready for adventure. For the first year, he'd rented a trailer in Presidio and traveled fairly extensively in Mexico. Then he'd been hired by the Texas chapter of the California-based environmental group, Bonis Avidus, which he'd explained to me was Latin for "Good Auspices." The group operated out of a rented building in Fort Davis in the next county north.

Crosse, hired to run the office, had shown remarkable rapport with the old-guard ranchers. Soon he was doing fieldwork, roaming the whole region to obtain conservation easements. So far, he'd had some success, I'd heard, and while opinion varied widely as to whether or not Bonis Avidus's environmental goals truly achieved what they claimed, no ill will seemed to attach to Crosse.

He came to the register to pay for his drink, his puppy-dog-friendly smile diminished to express polite concern for Clay. "Everyone seems truly outraged by his arrest," he said, a careful statement that avoided any commitment to such feelings on his part, since he neither knew us of long standing nor would he want to support the possible killer of his friend Daniel's father.

"Clay and I are grateful that our friends understand what it means for an innocent man to be accused of such a terrible crime," I said obliquely.

"I know I was shocked when I heard about it," Crosse said quizzically. "That day Daniel walked in here and said his daddy had been murdered, the first person I thought of was True Jackson."

"Jip Jackson's son? What could True have had against Zanjiv Mehendru?"

Crosse looked embarrassed. "I'm talking out of turn, I guess, but I don't see how it can hurt now if I tell it. Sooner or later everybody knows everything in a tight community like this. Daniel's daddy was the one who turned Jip Jackson in to the feds. I thought maybe True found out and went after the commissioner for putting his daddy in prison."

I was stunned and trying not to let it show. Until he'd been sentenced to federal prison a little over twelve months ago, Jip Jackson had been the only builder in Presidio. The Jackson family was one of the oldest, most respected in the region. Jip had been forced to sell the six-thousand-acre Jackson ranch to help pay his legal bills. No one knew who had blown the whistle on Jip Jackson for hiring illegals to work on the new Border Patrol headquarters on which he'd won the bid. All we knew was the Immigration and Naturalization Service, the Internal Revenue Service, and the Department of Labor had come after him and that he still owed taxes and interest on wages he'd falsified, underpaying the workers and pocketing the difference. If what Crosse told me was true, Mehendru's action had brought down a whole family.

"Someone called Zanjiv Mehendru a man of principle," I told Crosse, taking refuge in Mercedes Solar's words.

"The commissioner couldn't see anybody's way except his own. He wouldn't listen to reason, even from his own son."

"How is Daniel?" I asked.

"I haven't seen him in a while. His aunt is staying with him at the ranch."

"Do I know his aunt?" I said, thinking back to Mehendru's obituary and seeking easy confirmation of what I remembered vaguely about a half-sister who lived in Chihuahua City.

"Kim Garza," Crosse said. "Nice lady."

"I'm sure she is," I said. "Tell me, did Daniel worry when his father didn't come home the weekend he was killed?"

"The commissioner kept an apartment in El Paso, because of his job. He stayed there Monday through Friday. Daniel probably thought he was there or with his lady friend in Ojinaga."

"Mercedes Solar."

"You know her?" Crosse said, his eyes brightening with interest.

"She was at the hearing."

"I guess she'd have an interest in the outcome," he said.

"She wants justice done," I said, "and she seems to doubt that's what's happening right now."

"So you have her on your side," Crosse said.

"She wants to know the truth. She'd like Daniel to come and see her. I gather they've never met."

"I wouldn't know about that."

"I told her I'd pass along her request to Daniel. Under the circumstances, I can hardly tell him myself—"

"Sure, I'll tell him," Crosse said, "But I doubt it'll do much good. He's already hired a lawyer to fight her claiming anything from his dad's estate."

Intent on Clay's troubles, I hadn't thought through the obvious. As Mehendru's documented common-law wife, Solar would have a half-interest in his estate.

Having given me a lot to think about, Crosse paid and left. One by one, the remaining customers departed. By noon, the trading post was empty. I went to the back and tried to return Lisa Wharton's call from the day before, but got a busy signal. I unwrapped a portion of the carne asada Claudia had sent home with me the night before, forked two pieces of meat onto a piece of bread, and folded it over into a fat sandwich that I ate in three bites. Then I tried Lisa again.

"Is Clay coming back on the job next week?" she asked.

I explained what had happened at the hearing and heard the responding shock in Lisa's voice.

"Texana, I'm so sorry," she said. "This is unbelievable."

"It's a matter of time," I told her. "A couple of weeks, we hope. We can't do anything until the next hearing."

"I understand. I can handle Clay's emergency calls. I've only had one this week. But there's another problem I can't handle. Two cattle herds in Texas have been infected with TB and the Department of Agriculture has stripped the state of its tuberculosis-free status."

"This means what?"

"It means," Lisa said, "that no cattle can be shipped out of state until each animal has been tested and certified by a veterinarian. You know what that involves."

I did. Clay had often checked for TB on cattle crossing the border. It involved a two-step process conducted over a seventy-two-hour period during which the cattle had to remain penned. At three dollars a head, it was easy money for a veterinarian, but it was also time-consuming. For Clay, it would be no problem should local ranchers need him to check their herds. For Lisa, busy with her small-animal practice, spending an entire day testing a herd was an impossibility.

"How long does this quarantine last?" I said.

"Two years," Lisa said.

"If you get a call from one of Clay's clients wanting the testing," I said, "refer them back to me."

"I'm really sorry about this, especially now."

"It can't be helped. Can you hold out with the emergencies for, say, another week, while I make other arrangements?"

"Of course I can," she said.

I hung up and pulled out the area-wide telephone book. Clay had said Kevin Hayes owed him a favor. I hoped it was a big one. The Hayes Veterinary Clinic in Odessa has two partners who handle small and large animals. I explained the situation to Kevin as soon as his receptionist put him on the line.

"I've got just the person," he said. "There's a local boy, Mike Dodd. He worked as my assistant all through high school. His degree in veterinary medicine is brand-new and he knows he's got a place here in my clinic. I'll ask him how he'd like to see the big-sky country for a few weeks before he settles in."

"If he agrees, I'll have the guest room ready," I told Kevin.

"I think he'll jump at the idea," Kevin said.

I wrote a note to myself to dust the guest room and stuck it on the refrigerator. I wondered if Mike Dodd would agree as readily as Kevin thought to staying in the home of an accused murderer. Polvo and our friends around the county might know Clay to be innocent. The rest of the world didn't.

EIGHTEEN

Deputy Sheriff Dennis Bustamante's handsome face wasn't wearing its usual smile as he came in the front door that afternoon to pay for the fill-up of the department's Grand Marquis.

"Everybody in my area's really angry about what's happening to Clay," he said, signing the ticket for thirty-two dollars and forty cents' worth of unleaded.

By his area, Dennis meant the southern half of the county, that part that lies below the Border Patrol checkpoint on Highway 67 from Marfa. The checkpoint divides two different climate zones—high desert grasslands versus desert scrub—and two different mentalities—Anglo versus frontera. Lots of the folks in Marfa have never been to Presidio and wouldn't dream of crossing over to Ojinaga. The ones who have tend to view us as quaint or foreign. We find both perspectives patronizing.

I slipped the ticket book back into the drawer and asked, "What can you tell me about True Jackson?"

"We played six-man football together in high school. He has a wife and two kids. He teaches English as a second language at the high school and saved like a miser to buy up those fields by the river for his organic onion business. I heard that True borrowed against his land to help pay his dad's legal expenses."

"I thought they sold the family ranch to pay the lawyers."

"They did," Dennis said. "To that environmental bunch, but it wasn't enough. Jip wanted the land kept intact, so he took a lower offer after they promised him they'd honor his wishes."

"But I heard that Bonis Avidus sold off the Jackson Ranch in sections."

Dennis nodded. "You heard right. They subdivided it a week after the contract closed. The worst thing is, they got almost as much for one section as they paid for the whole place. It broke Jip's heart that they cut the ranch up like that. True was so mad on his dad's account that I thought he'd have a heart attack. He talked to a lawyer about suing them, but the contract his dad signed didn't specify keeping the land in one piece."

"Did the Jacksons ever find out who blew the whistle on Jip?" I asked.

"No. For months after Jip was found guilty, everybody in Presidio speculated on who it might be, but we never figured it out."

"Do you think True might have known who did it?"

"You're not thinking True turned in his own daddy?"

"Not at all," I assured him. "Someone suggested to me that True might have held a grudge against Zanjiv Mehendru."

"The River Master turned Jip in to the feds?"

"I don't know if it's fact," I told him.

"I'll bet it is," Dennis said emphatically. "That man couldn't stay out of other people's business. Like with poor old Flaco Ordaz. Forty years he's kept a garbage dump on his place upriver 'cause it's a hundred and twenty-three miles to the nearest landfill. Nobody bothered the old man until Mehendru bought the Sloe Ranch next door and goes over to introduce himself to Mr. Ordaz. He spots the dump and asks Ordaz about it. The old man thinks Mehendru is asking because he wants to start a dump on his place, so he tells him how his son-in-law, who works for the county, brings out a backhoe and a dozer once a year, buries the old dump site and digs a new one. He even offers to get the son-in-law to help. Mehendru goes straight from the old man's place to the telephone. He raised such a stink that the precinct commissioner had to dun Ordaz's son-in-law for the hourly costs of using county equipment on private land. Poor guy had to take out a loan to pay it off."

"But the closest private bulldozer operator is in the next county," I said. "If the county commissioners didn't let us use their dozers, we wouldn't have any ranch roads. The men do the work on their own time, after all."

"And everybody knows it," Dennis said. "Even Mehendru. But it wasn't by the book, and that's how the man's mind worked. If you're hoping to corral everyone he came up on the wrong side of, you're going to need extra fencing."

"Clay's facing a prison term for something he didn't do. I have to try."

"What can I do to help?" Dennis asked.

"Find out if True Jackson had an alibi for the Saturday night Mehendru was shot."

It was nearly five when Dennis left. I closed as usual at six, had a cold dinner, exercised Phobe and Jefe outside, coming in just at dark. I took an antihistamine to help me sleep and went to bed at ten.

I dozed restlessly until midnight, each wakeful moment a fresh worry about Clay and what might happen. Finally, I turned on my side, listening to the faint night sounds through the open window, watching the shifting patterns of moonlight on the floor, searching the shadows for peace of mind.

After what seemed like hours of sleeplessness, I eased from

under the light blanket, trying not to wake the sleeping bobcat and Jefe, curled up by her side. I took my robe from the chair and put it on, went through to the great room, switched on the floor lamp behind the couch, and headed for the kitchen. As soon as the refrigerator door opened, I heard Phobe's feet hit the floor in the bedroom. I poured a glass of milk for me and put a little milk in Phobe's and Jefe's bowls just as they padded in. While they lapped, I found Mercedes Solar's book where I'd left it on the shelf by the back door, and carried it with me to the couch. The lapping sounds ended and Phobe jumped up on the couch and flopped down across my feet. I reached down with one hand and scooped Jefe onto my lap.

I opened the book. Solar had dedicated *En Tierra de Nod* to Z.M. When I read the epigram, I realized why the title had seemed familiar. It was from Genesis. "And Cain went out from the presence of the Lord, and dwelt in the land of Nod."

The book was brief, only one hundred pages. It was five minutes past four when I finished the story of a boy born on a farm in central Mexico. As he watches, his drunken father, playing matador in the bull pen, is trampled to death. Unable to support his mother and three sisters, the twelve-year-old persuades a neighbor who has crossed the border illegally many times to take him on the next trip. The boy finds work in a landscape nursery in El Paso, moves on to a cannery, sorting green and red peppers. He shares a rented room with five other men. He mails most of his paycheck home to his mother. For five long years, this is his life, until one day the loneliness and longing for home become too great to bear and he makes his way back across the border and finally home, only to find his mother has died in his absence. Two of his sisters have left home to cross the border for work and the third has married. Her husband has taken over the farm. Unable to return to his former life, the boy tries to cross the border again, only to be caught by the Border Patrol and sent back.

I closed the book and set it on the floor beside the couch.

Mercedes Solar had lived and worked in both Juárez and El Paso, a mujer transfronteriza, a woman at home on either side of the border. Or was she? Was the book autobiographical, the lost boy, exiled from both worlds, she herself? Or was he someone she had known, someone living an exile of the soul? Zanjiv Mehendru?

NINETEEN

Sunday, April 21

There is no place I'd rather be in the early morning than sitting on the front porch of the trading post. With a cup of coffee at hand, I settled back against the cushioned chair and watched Phobe and Jefe enjoying the short-lived cool. The quiet was immense.

Nor did anything disturb the eye. Beyond the greenbelt, everything around is low-growing and compact. The only signs of life require an experienced vision: the bulky, dense shadow of a horned owl in the highest branches of the tallest tree; the low, fleeting, rufous shape of a late-roaming coyote; the swift, soundless flight of a roadrunner with a lizard in its bill, gliding from ground to nest.

Scents, too, are muted, faint, and familiar: a musky aroma where some javelina has rubbed against the rocks that line the porch; the minty fragrance of creosote bush that the afternoon heat will burn away; and beneath it all, the thick, clean smell of the night-cooled earth.

A frantic squeaking disturbed the Edenic image as Phobe toyed with a captured rat before finally making the killing bite that breaks the neck. She carried it in her mouth, limp and dangling, and dropped it at Jefe's feet. The Chihuahua sniffed the offering, barked at it, then rolled on it. Phobe jumped on Jefe. While the bobcat was distracted, I went to remove the rat before she could eat it, lifting it by the tail and tossing it into the brush, where later some keen-eyed black vulture would find it. The desert wastes nothing.

Resettled on the porch, I drank my coffee and regretted that it was far too early for a whiskey. Saturday had been brutal. Busy with customers, I'd worried all day about what Jack Raff had said when he dropped by after his trip to see Clay on Friday:

"Trouble is, he has nothing to do but worry. And it's never quiet in the cells, Clay says. Even at night, they've got radios going, so he isn't getting much rest."

Jack had taken Clay a stack of magazines and a couple of historical novels by Patrick O'Brian. Today, he would accompany me on the two-hour family visit. He'd already told the warden that he was Clay's cousin, "fabricating in a good cause," as he called it. He was going to bring his traveling chess set so that he and Clay could begin a game. I appreciated the gesture, but I didn't believe Clay would be able to think strategy any more than he could concentrate on reading in that place, with the very real possibility of spending months there if the hearings dragged out. If he was found guilty—I could count on the fingers of one hand the times we'd been separated from each other by more than the length of a busy day.

I pushed the thought away and resorted to action. Pulling a four-foot length of twine and a small ball out of my pocket, I went to play with Phobe and Jefe. The pair felt my anxiety.

Phobe had roamed the trading post all night, staring out the windows in turn, as if watching for Clay's pickup. Every time a customer came in, Jefe ran to the door in anticipation and turned away in disappointment when it wasn't Clay.

When I'd worn the pair down a little, we went inside and had breakfast. Afterward, I packed fresh clothes for another week for Clay, more bottled water, some snack foods, and a small electric fan. No matter what Clay said about not wanting me to make the long drive to visit daily, I wasn't going to miss any of the family days.

I boiled some eggs for Clay's lunch and while they cooled I ran the vacuum. Just as I cut it off, the telephone rang.

"The night of the murder," Dennis Bustamante said without preamble, "True Jackson and a bunch of his friends drove down to Terlingua to listen to some music and drink a few beers at the Starlight Theatre."

"That was fast work," I said, referring to how quickly he had honored my request to check True out. Terlingua was a reborn ghost town near the western entrance to Big Bend National Park and roughly as far from Ojinaga downriver as Polvo was upriver.

"I talked to True for quite a while," Dennis said. "He has some information I think you should hear. Are you going to see Clay today?"

"Yes."

"I thought you would," Dennis said. "I told True you might stop by the farm headquarters afterward, say about two-thirty. He said he'd be around."

"What am I supposed to talk to him about?" I asked.

"Irrigation," Dennis said. I heard the crackle of the dispatcher's voice in the background, then Dennis said, "I've got to roll. Good luck."

I put the vacuum away, went back to the kitchen counter and chopped the eggs, added mayo, salt, pepper, and a strong dash of Tabasco Green Pepper Sauce. I spread the mixture on bread, cut and wrapped the sandwiches, changed into a clean cotton shirt, got my keys, carried the cooler and an extra folding chair out to the pickup, and drove to Jack Raff's adobe.

The house is a mile and a half off the road, about a third of the way to Presidio. Jack's pickup was parked nearby, with a fat red tabby cat curled in sleep on the hood. The wooden door and shutters that covered the adobe's windows at night were open to the daylight. Jack had heard me coming and stood in the yard, which was distinguished from the surrounding landscape by a fence of prickly pear so ancient that its lower branches were thickened and horny like bark.

"That looks impregnable," I said, getting out. The slamming door caused the cat to open its eyes to slits, but at the sound of Jack's voice greeting me, it closed them again, secure in its world.

"Keeps the coyotes out," Jack said, opening the wooden gate he'd wedged into the wall of cacti. "Come in and look around, while I get the chess set together."

In Jack Raff's former rectory in Polvo, every available surface, including the floor, had been littered with magazines, newspapers, books, and almost anything that most households kept in closets. This room was as unlike that as could be imagined. Plastered in a cool lime green, the walls were bare except for a row of landscape photographs. The only furnishings were a round dining table and four chairs, an armchair upholstered in brown twill, and a brass floor lamp.

"This is restful," I said when he came back from the next room with the chest set in its box. "The last time I saw this place, it was falling in and full of rattlesnakes."

"I had to relocate a den of them before I could clean up and patch up," Jack said, "but all in all, I think it turned out okay. You ready to go?"

"Ready," I said.

The journey went faster with company and conversation. Clay met us just inside the prison gates. He smiled and shook Jack's hand, and made small talk on the way to his cell. This was my husband nervous and upset. When things are normal, when Clay is happy and relaxed, he is quiet, almost slothlike in his ease.

Jack set up the chess board on the milk carton while I unfolded the extra chair, unwrapped sandwiches, opened a couple of bottles of water. While we ate, with Jack keeping up conversation largely on his own, I watched Clay. He was never still. He jackhammered his legs incessantly as he sat on the cot, and when he stood he rubbed his left arm with his right hand, up and down.

"Does your arm hurt?" I finally asked.

"What?" he said, looking down at his arm and his own hand as if he'd never seen them before. "No."

Snippets of the conversations of sixty prisoners and their families filled the long void in ours.

Finally, Clay said, "Manuel, the man in the next cell, has been waiting eight months for his pre-trial hearing. He stole a bicycle. A man named Victor tells me he's been here nearly a year since his hearing. He's accused of shooting a neighbor's donkey. He says the prosecutor claims to be collecting evidence for the trial, but that he has it in for Victor over a remark he made at the hearing."

"You can't give up, Clay," I said.

"We've only started to fight this," Jack said. "You have a lot of people on your side."

"The only person who matters is the prosecutor," Clay said flatly. "I'm in here because a witness lied and the magistrate knows it. So what am I supposed to think, except that I'm going to be found guilty no matter what."

He was right. Unless we found some way out, he'd be in here for years. I tried to encourage him, telling him about Tito Berg, emphasizing his connections and influence. I'd intended talking with Berg first, making sure he'd take the case, but Clay needed some hope. If Berg failed us, I'd find someone else. I'd have to.

Jack excused himself and left us. I watched as he moved across the hot prison yard to the corner where the warden's father sat in his wheelchair, shaded by an umbrella held by a prisoner. I moved across to the cot, sat down by Clay, and took his hand in mine, our shoulders touching.

Too soon, the loudspeaker announced the time and I got up to go. As Jack and I neared the gates, Warden Martinez, with Zapata on his shoulder, motioned to me.

Good afternoon, Señora Jones," he said, as I approached the shadowed doorway where he stood. "May we speak?"

"Certainly, Warden," I said.

"Please, in my office; it is more private," he said.

Jack said he'd wait by the gate. I followed the warden down the hall and into the office. He closed the door behind me, pulled out a chair for me, and went to sit on the corner of his desk, lifting the cat from his shoulder as he did so and placing it on the desk, where it sprawled comfortably.

"Zapata has gained some weight," I said.

The warden smiled broadly and rubbed the cat's belly. "He is a new animal since your husband treated him. That's what gave me the idea."

"Idea?"

"Your husband tells me he has a van fitted out as a mobile clinic and operating room for small animals and that he used to take this van sometimes to Presidio and hold his clinic there. We have many pets in Ojinaga," the warden said. "I think it would be possible for you to bring this van here to the municipal courtyard, where it would be safe from thieves and vandals. Then your husband can work. Under my supervision, of course."

"Of course," I said, grasping where he was going. "Your time would have to be compensated for—"

"A small amount, say half of each fee."

"One third, plus lifetime free care for Zapata," I said.

He bounced off the desk and extended his hand. "Señora, we have a deal."

TWENTY

Jack thought I should talk with True Jackson alone, so I dropped him off at the Three Palms coffee shop.

Following O'Reilly Street, I drove on until it became Millington, then turned onto Ranch Road 170 southeast past old Fort Leaton, built in 1846 by a scalp hunter hired by the Mexican government. Three miles beyond the fort was a one-story, flat-roofed building of ugly beige brick with a sign at the gate that read JACKSON FARMS. I parked in the heat-radiating cement lot and went inside, where the rotating drum fan of a water cooler roared as it blasted out damp air.

A strongly built man with skin browned by the sun sat at a metal desk punching a calculator and writing down the resultant figures on a sheet of paper in front of him. He wore a white short-sleeved shirt, faded jeans, and scuffed boots that I could see sticking out on the far side of the desk. His green baseball cap had a "Jackson Farms" logo in red lettering against a white onion-shaped patch.

"Mr. Jackson? I'm Texana Jones," I said loudly, to overcome the air-conditioner noise.

He looked up, shoved back his chair, and got up, reaching out an incredibly callused hand for me to shake. "Call me True. I've seen you around, but I don't think we've ever met. I know your husband, though. He doctors my kids' dogs when he brings his van to Presidio. Let's go outside where we can hear ourselves." He led the way, not out the door I'd entered, but down a hallway, past rest rooms and a big kitchen, and out the back door.

For as far as I could see, the broad river plain stretched sandy and empty.

"This time of year," True said, stopping, "those fields should be filled with rows of sweet onions ready for the pickers."

"The drought?" I asked.

"That's the excuse," True said. He got to his feet and gestured toward the river. "Look at it. It's just a big, dry ditch." He turned and gave me a steady, sizing-up kind of look." And the reason it's dry is because Chihuahua State is hoarding Rio Conchos water."

"I understand how you feel," I said, looking at the thin ribbon of water running down the middle of a wide, dry bed. "The land around Polvo used to be farmed, before El Paso swallowed all the water," I said. "Now, we're the forgotten part of the river. The only time our part of the Rio Grande flows more than a trickle is when we have a few inches of rain."

He nodded, pleased with my understanding. "You and your husband are having a bit of trouble," he said softly.

"Yes."

His eyes turned back to the horizon. "Let's sit down over here," he said, leading the way to a grouping of plastic chairs, the kind you buy at discount stores. There must have been twenty of them scattered around under the three old mesquites that had been left to grow at the edge of the closest field.

"Shade for the pickers while they ate lunch," True explained, "when the fields provided jobs instead of dust."

I took a chair next to him and turned it so I could see his face while we talked.

"You know about my daddy, of course," True said, no hint of self-pity in his voice. "Dennis told me it was Mehendru that turned him in. He did it to ease my mind. I thought it was one of our office workers, people I liked, but I've spent every day since thinking one of them was the whistle-blower."

Behind us, a man came out of the building, calling for True.

"Excuse me a minute," he said, getting up and going over. He talked with the man for a few minutes, then returned.

"Sorry, I'm arranging an equipment auction. Anyway, Like I was saying, everybody knows my daddy is in prison. What they don't know is what it's done to him. He's spent all his life outdoors. Now he's in a cell twenty-four hours a day and it's killing him. The prison doctors have him on Xanax for panic attacks and on Prozac for depression. His blood pressure is sky-high and he spends half the time in the hospital ward. I wouldn't wish prison on any man."

I needed a Xanax myself after True's remarks, but I knew he meant to let me know he understood what Clay faced better than most.

True turned his eyes away from the barren fields and directly at me. "Your husband helped Daddy out right after everything blew up on him."

"I didn't know that," I said. "But then, Clay keeps quiet about most people he helps."

"Daddy was going to sell off his cattle as a down payment for his lawyer, but he had a cow that tested positive for brucellosis. Clay tested the rest of the herd, two hundred head, and wouldn't take any pay. I figure what I'm going to say is owed to you."

"Dennis said I should ask you about irrigation," I told him.

"Around here," he said, "pulling stalled trucks out of the river used to be a growth industry until Mexico dried up the water. Because of that, I'm out of business, like every other grower. Downstream there are hundreds more worse off than me, because they don't just depend on the river for irrigation. It's their drinking water, too. The Rio Grande Valley is on its knees. The growers have lost more than a billion dollars and thirty thousand jobs. It's barren down there," True said, "on both sides of the river. But you take a drive over into Chihuahua State and look at the Rio Conchos Basin east of Chihuahua City, like I did. It's green farmland in the middle of desert. I saw pecan fields using flood irrigation, alfalfa fields, and a dairy with thirty thousand cows."

I remembered the green lawns in Ojinaga and Mercedes Solar washing down the dusty walls of her house, and sat up straighter in my chair. "I knew the newspaper said that Mexico wasn't honoring the water treaty, but I thought it was because of the drought."

"We're all hurting from lack of rainfall, sure," True said, "but the Rio Conchos in Chihuahua isn't dependent on rainfall in the desert. It gets so much runoff from rains in the Sierra Madre Occidental that Ojinaga is the only district in Mexico without irrigation limits. The water that fills the Rio Grande Valley's irrigation ditches is controlled by releases from dams in northern Mexico. Under the water treaty we guarantee that Mexico gets a water supply from the Colorado River and they guarantee us the same for the Rio Conchos."

My assumption had been that the long drought had depleted the Rio Conchos enough to force Mexico to hoard the water that should be flowing into the Rio Grande. Now True was telling me otherwise.

"Mexico started falling back on releasing water ten years ago," True said. "For the past four years, they've stopped altogether. Now they owe the Rio Grande more than four hundred and eighty billion gallons of water. The campesinos down in Tamaulipas State are hurting every bit as much as the farmers on the U.S. side. Between Reynosa and Matamoros they had to pull nearly five hundred million acres out of production; now they're lobbying Mexico's federal officials to honor the water treaty and force the governor of Chihuahua to release the water."

"Will it help?" I asked.

"The officials in Mexico City just keep saying the water isn't available, but the governor of Chihuahua State told reporters that the government was building a pipeline to divert more water from the Luis Leon Reservoir for the maquiladora plants in Chihuahua City. There are those who say the water is being diverted for the opium poppy growers." True stared ahead, not at the fields, but the river—what was left of it, beyond. "This part of the Rio Grande has been inhabited for twelve thousand years because it had water. Now, in less than half a lifetime, the water may dry up altogether."

"Is there any alternative?" I said.

True laughed caustically. "If the International Boundary and Water Commission had done their job and respected the treaty, there'd be water enough for everybody," True said. "I think if anybody wanted to kill the River Master, it would be a grower who had to stand by helpless and watch generations of his family's work blow away in dust."

TWENTY-ONE

Wednesday, April 24

I drove the van equipped as a small-animal emergency sur-
gery and veterinary clinic—the "vetmobile," as Clay calls it—
to Ojinaga, with Jack Raff following in my pickup to bring
me home.

The look on Clay's face as the van pulled into the municipal courtyard lightened my heart. I parked it by the warden's
brown '68 Buick convertible.

The warden was there with his father, a prisoner pushing
the wheelchair into the sparse shade provided by the only
tree. Warden Martinez seemed delighted as Clay showed him
the surgical table that pulled down from the wall of the van,
the tiny refrigeration unit for keeping vaccines cooled, the
miniature lab area for diagnostic work, and all the other special details Clay had ordered built-in.

"Truly amazing," the warden said. "My idea is going to be very successful."

Jack and I visited with Clay for a few minutes, long enough for him to go over his supplies and give me a list of things to bring on the Sunday visit, such as extra rabies and distemper vaccines.

Jack dropped me at the trading post. There was a white Honda Civic parked in front and a sandy-haired young man in wire-rim glasses sitting on the porch.

"I'm Mike Dodd," he said, getting to his feet as I walked up. "You must be Texana."

"Kevin Haynes speaks very highly of you," I said. "I'm so grateful you're willing to stand in for my husband. Come in."

He stopped just inside the door to look around at the crowded shelves and in particular at Phobe perched on the stacks of packaged Dickies work shirts.

"I thought Kevin was pulling my leg about the bobcat," he said.

Phobe had turned her black-tufted ears and her round golden eyes in our direction. I introduced her to Mike. He scratched her back. She yawned and rolled over and stretched. Mike took the hint and rubbed her stomach. Jefe ran in, her tail going like a metronome.

"This is lordly company," Mike said.

I showed him around the trading post and our quarters, then took him out to the guest room we'd added on the southwest side. It's three hundred square feet, including the bath, and has an entrance off the front porch. Mike fetched a travel bag and small suitcase from his car.

"This is nice," he said politely, though genuine pleasure showed in his eyes as he looked around the room. I'd painted the walls what I call Frida Kahlo blue. The bed and desk were light pine.

I left Mike to unpack and unwind a bit before lunch. When he was ready, I grilled hamburgers. While he watched Phobe and Jefe play, Mike told me about himself. His father was a doctor, his mother a lawyer. He had a brother in graduate school and a sister in pre-med at the University of Texas.

After lunch I took him out to the clinic, explaining the arrangement Clay and I had discussed. In addition to room and board, Mike would get the fees for all the calls he made. I showed him the list of Clay's rates posted on the wall. Last, I gave him the list of clients who'd left messages the past few days.

"Tomorrow's soon enough to get started," I said. "Hugger Baines is first on the list. He has a mule with an inflamed tendon, but he said it wasn't urgent. You might call on Gwen Masters tomorrow. One of her cows is off its feed."

"How about I go now," he said eagerly. "Should I call first?"

"They'll both be at home," I said.

I had a map showing most of the ranches and county roads. I marked it for him and gave him the keys to Clay's pickup. "The drill is, always check your gas gauge. Fill up at the pumps out front," I told him. "You'll get used to having to fill up almost every time you come in. We're miles from everything, including each other."

As I came back in from watching him drive away, the telephone rang.

"Good news," Enrique said, and the tone of his voice indicated that substance supported his words. "Tito Berg will meet with you."

"When and where?"

"He's juggling several cases, so you'll have to go to Chihuahua. He has some free time at three next Tuesday. His office is at eight-thirteen Ocampo."

"I'll be there," I almost shouted.

TWENTY-TWO

Tuesday, April 30

From the trading post, the drive to Chihuahua City takes four and a half hours.

Chihuahua's money once came from mining, cattle, and timber. Now, the encircling sierras are bare of trees and the mines are played out. The cattle ranches remain and many of the men you see on the streets are dressed in Western shirts, jeans, straw cowboy hats, and boots, but most work in the maquiladora industry, foreign-owned assembly plants that are now the city's biggest commercial enterprise.

Driving through the ordinary-looking business district, you might be anywhere, but in the heart of the city, where most of the municipal offices and museums are located, the massive grandeur of nineteenth-century architecture gives Chihuahua distinction.

I parked in the lot belonging to the Hotel San Juan on

Calle Victoria, southwest of the Plaza de Armas. When Clay and I had first visited here fifteen years ago, the room rates had been $12.50 for a double with a private bath. Today, the manager quoted me the single rate of $32.50 almost apologetically. I dumped my bag in the room and went back out to the street. It was two-fifteen.

I walked back toward the plaza and turned right onto Ocampo Street. Berg's office was in one of the newer buildings, ugly outside but more comfortable inside than the historic structures.

I took the stairs to the second floor. Past a polished door, a handsome young male secretary asked if I'd like coffee or Perrier while I waited. "Nothing," I said.

I sat enveloped in an oversized lime green armchair and stared at the red walls dominated by two paintings by Francisco Toledo, one of Mexico's greatest artists. I began to doubt whether I could pay Tito Berg's fees.

I hadn't expected Berg to be on time, but neither did I expect what the secretary said after reading an e-mail.

"Señora Jones, licenciado Berg is delayed at home. He wonders if you would care to join him there. He's sending his car for you."

"Of course," I said. Fifteen minutes later, a gray-haired man dressed neatly in a white shirt and black pants entered the waiting room from a doorway somewhere down the hall and greeted the secretary, who introduced him as Berg's driver. I accompanied him downstairs to a courtyard where orange lines marked numbered parking spaces. The driver held open the door of a glossy black Mercedes in space number one. I climbed in, fastened my seat belt, and tried to relax as we drove through the arched gateway into the city traffic.

In minutes, we were out of the historic district, heading southwest. We passed through a section of renovated Victorian mansions to a new neighborhood beyond. We drove down a wide street past homes of varying architectural types but equal in size and lavishness, with lawns like golfing greens shaded by blooming jacaranda trees. The driver slowed, turning into the driveway of a modern slab of a house, its severe exterior a stuccoed red wall broken only by the wide front door and one square window high on the right, just above the black metal of the double garage doors.

The driver pressed a remote control, the garage door rolled up, and the Mercedes rolled in. He opened my door, then moved around me to hold an inner door that led into the house.

"Please come this way," he said. We moved down a white plastered hallway of generous proportions, past several doors, and up a flight of narrow steps painted cobalt blue to the second level. He tapped on a door and a masculine voice said, "Come."

"Señora Jones," the driver announced before nodding to me and leaving, closing the door behind him.

A cigar in his fingers, Tito Berg stood up from his austere desk and smiled at me with the whitest teeth I've ever seen. He was larger than I expected, at least six feet, and thick-waisted without being flabby. He wore jeans and a white guayabera shirt. His feet were encased in soft suede moccasins.

"Please, sit," he said. "Does the smoke bother you?"

"Not at all. My father smokes cigars."

He looked pleased. "Would you care for one?"

"No, thank you."

Leaning back in my chair, I took in the deceptive simplicity of Berg's office. The only object on the desk, other than a blue folder, was a framed black-and-white photograph of a middle-aged couple in clothes of the forties. The woman, with her big, soft eyes and even features, looked strikingly like Berg, though she was younger in the picture than he was now.

"Your parents?" I asked, nodding at the photograph.

"They immigrated from Germany before I was born," Berg said. "My father was an artist. I take after my mother. She'd have made a good lawyer. My father died a few years ago. My mother still lives in their house, one of the old Victorian homes you passed on the way here. She can no longer manage the stairs, but she refuses to install an elevator."

The smoke from his cigar clouded the air. Berg reached across to the credenza and switched on an air filter that sat on top. "This is the only room in the house in which my wife allows me to smoke," he said.

The room was white and flooded with natural light from a wide window high on the left-hand wall. A painting of an Indian woman with an armful of calla lilies gave the room color.

Berg, following my gaze, said, "An original Diego Rivera. A gift from a grateful client whose funds were otherwise tied up at the time."

And worth more than Clay and I would earn in a lifetime. I thought about the single piece of artwork we owned, an Andrew Wyeth print of a sleeping dog that I'd ordered for Clay's office from a pet-supply catalog, and figured Berg wouldn't like it anyway. I was in way over my head here, but Clay needed the best and on the drive over I'd thought of a way to make it possible financially.

"I've been looking over the newspaper stories of your husband's case," Berg said, balancing his cigar on the glass ashtray on his desk and touching the folder in front of him. "Vera tells me there are some highly questionable things happening regarding your husband's detention. No one, not the state police, the prosecutor, the assistant attorney general, nor that rascal attorney general Vascón, would talk to him about the case against your husband. So many dogs after one poor little bone." He stared off into the space above my head. "Curious, isn't it."

He picked up his cigar, puffed, and brought his focus back to me. "You know how our system works? A magistrate single-handedly directs the collection of the evidence, hears witnesses, and decides guilt or innocence. It's a system perfected over seventy-one years of one-party rule to favor the criminals and drug traffickers who have money enough to intimidate or buy the one man who can change their fate." Berg rolled the cigar in his fingers. "I've decided to accept this case. Can you afford me?"

"How much are we talking about?"

"I charge in dollars, because I work in dollars," he said. "By that, I mean you get the best. I'll defend Clay like a pit bull. For this case, my fee is one hundred thousand, plus expenses," he said.

I took a deep breath to help force the words out. "I can manage that," I said.

He smiled and rubbed his hands. "This is good. I'm inclined to think your husband's arrest is due to politics. Alfonso Carmin, the prosecutor, is being pressured by José Cabello, the assistant attorney general in charge of the case. He's being pushed by his boss, the attorney general. Benito Vascón can't afford any more high-profile, unsolved cases. He already has his hands full trying to solve the Juárez serial killings, the murder of the family of the forensic scientist who was studying the women's murders, and the attempted murder of the governor."

"But why Clay?"

"The judiciales had to arrest someone. My guess is that since the victim was a nortéamericano of some importance, it seemed best to them to have the killer be a nortéamericano of, forgive me, less importance. I'll call Benito and ask a few questions." Berg showed his bright smile again. "He'll lie to me, of course, but lies can be as telling as the truth."

TWENTY-THREE

I had Berg's driver drop me at the Biblioteca Miguel Hidalgo, which was only six blocks from my hotel. The helpful woman at the reference desk brought me the back copies of *El Diario de Chihuahua*. I took the thick stack of newspapers to a table and spread them out. The dates covered the two weeks immediately following the murder of Zanjiv Mehendru.

I found four news stories about the killing and its lack of progress and one feature on Mehendru's life. All more or less mirrored the coverage I'd read in the *International*, except that clearly he had been highly esteemed on this side of the Rio Grande.

In the feature detailing his life, I found one interesting paragraph, subheaded "One of Our Own."

Born in the United States but raised in Juárez, Mehendru identified with Mexico. "I consider myself bicultural," he said when he was appointed in 1998 to head the United States Sector of the International Boundary and Water Commission. Many here in Chihuahua considered Mehendru an American success story, but a Mexican by sympathy and emotion. His ties to Chihuahua ran deep. He was the half-brother of Arturo Blancas, CEO of Grupo Prima, the Chihuahua-based company which, among other holdings, owns Cervecería Optima, which makes fifty percent of the beer sold in this country, including the Pájaro and Amigo labels.

I took the newspaper to the copy machine, printed the feature, and handed in the newspapers to the librarian just as the library's public-address system announced closing time. I asked if I might stay long enough to use the single computer terminal for a few minutes, but she told me to come back tomorrow.

Clutching the smeary copy of the newspaper story, I hurried along the pavement, crowded with workers going home for the day. Did Mehendru's Chihuahuan connection have anything to do with his siding with Mexico on the water question? Had his family stood to gain financially?

CASA DE EMPEÑOS read the yellow-and-blue sign hanging over the sidewalk. I glanced in the pawnshop's window and saw, hooked up on a desk by the caged register, a computer. I folded up the copy of the news story, placed it in the pocket of my skirt, went in and walked straight to the computer. The screen saver pulsed with the recurrent image of a charging bull. I had my hand on the mouse when the pawnbroker came around from his cage.

"You like this?" the big-featured man said. "I'll make you a special price."

"I'd like to check it out. Make sure it works," I said.

"It works fine, I guarantee."

"I'm sure it does," I said. "Would you let me go to one Web site?"

"I'm in business to sell," he said insistently. "You want to use it, buy something." He stretched his arms to encompass the entire inventory.

I looked around, saw a display case of rings marked one hundred pesos each, roughly ten dollars. "One of these," I said.

The pawnbroker unlocked the glass top, lifted it. I reached in and picked up the one closest at hand, a big ring, the top shaped into an elaborately detailed saddle. I paid and slipped the ring over my middle finger, the only one it would fit. The pawnbroker smiled, waved a hand at the computer, and said, "Go ahead." He went back into his cage.

I logged on, typing in "www.grupoprima.com."

I'd guessed the obvious for the Web site and was right. The Web page listed Grupo Prima's directors, including not only Arturo Blancas, the CEO, but Aurelio Blancas, chairman emeritus, Eduardo Blancas, director general of ALPHA, and Kimberly Blancas de Garza, director general of CINSA.

The company's history was capsuled:

In 1890, Francisco Blancas and Felipe Carrillo joined forces to establish a brewery, Cervecería Optimo. The business foundation they laid was the cornerstone for what was to become a major industrial giant headquartered in Chihuahua and Juárez. The key to their success was their visionary approach toward the vertical integration of their companies' products. In 1903, the partners established a plant to manufacture crowns for their bottles. In 1909, they inaugurated a new glass plant to make their own bottles. In 1942, when Juan Blancas assumed leadership of Optimo, the company built a steel foundry to provide a steady supply for the crowns. This was followed by a paper-manufacturing plant for cartons and labels, as well as printing facilities. Later, a plant was added to convert the spent grain used in the brewing process into cattle feed for a beef-production facility. In 1979, Juan's eldest son, Aurelio, bought out the remaining Carillo interests. In 1989, he named his son Arturo as CEO, turning the reins of the business over to him. During the next ten years, the company diversified still more, including the creation of new products under the name Grupo Prima.

I clicked on to the chart showing the company's holdings. Grupo Prima was not only a consortium of breweries that had won prestigious gold medals at the Munich Oktoberfest, but owned twelve other companies in what was referred to as the brewery group. The principals and directors—read the Blancases and their extended family—also owned majority shares in ALPHA, with five operating divisions focused on PVC pipe, fibers, water-treatment plants, and bottled water; CINSA, a chemical powerhouse; and VITA, with over one hundred companies manufacturing such things as plastics and electronic devices for various industry and consumer applications.

I pulled the news story copy out of my pocket, begged a pen from the pawnbroker, and made some notes. I didn't know if there was any significance to what I'd just learned in terms of Mehendru's murder or Clay's arrest, but these people had power and money enough to pressure an attorney general, let alone a magistrate.

At the hotel, I went straight to the restaurant, ordered a margarita, and indulged myself in three of the eight kinds of tacos served. Back in my room, I took off my suit and hung it on the hanger hooked over the back of the door, put on my robe, and got into bed. My last thought was of Mercedes Solar. She had to know that Zanjiv Mehendru's stepfather was one of the most powerful men in Chihuahua State. In Mexico. Why hadn't she told me?

TWENTY-FOUR

Wednesday, May 1

I needed to see Tito Berg again before I left Chihuahua, so I hung around the hotel restaurant, making my third cup of coffee last.

At nine, I checked out of Hotel San Juan, retrieved my pickup from the locked parking area, and drove to Berg's office building. The young secretary was behind the desk in the red-walled reception room looking as if he'd never left. He smiled up at me and said it was possible for me to see licenciado Berg as soon as he arrived.

Thirty minutes later, Berg ushered me into his office. If there were file cabinets, memos, or the stacks of documents so neccesary in a world where paper talks, they were kept out of sight. The glass-topped desk had only a humidor and a large ashtray on it. A painting, this one an abstract splash of vivid color, adorned the wall behind the desk.

"I have something to show you," I said, handing over the copy of the news story I'd made at the library.

It only took him an instant to read the single, important sentence I'd underlined. "I must read *El Diario* more often," he said. "I had no idea this man Mehendru was part of the Blancases' extended family." He leaned back in the molded leather chair and gazed thoughtfully into space. "Do you know how grupos are set up?" he asked, swiveling his chair to face me across the wide desk.

"They're like holding companies, I guess."

"Not exactly," Berg said. "In your country, a conglomerate is a parent company that owns subsidiary enterprises bound to them by legal stipulations. The ties that bind grupos are entirely familial."

"That explains the list of Grupo Prima's directors," I said. "All Blancases."

Berg nodded. "It means not only do the companies have the same operating philosophy, they share the same channels of distribution, marketing intelligence, everything. What makes the grupos strong is their source of ready cash for growth and acquisition. Every grupo owns either a bank or an insurance company, or both."

I was beginning to see where he might be going and it scared me. "Perfect for money laundering," I said.

"Recycled narco-dollars propel huge amounts of private investment," Berg said. "It's said that it was drug money that bought out the Carrillo partners in Cervecería Optima. Aurelio Blancas got into drug trafficking as a young man in Juárez. In a world of brutal men, he was known to be particularly brutal, a positive attribute among his kind. When his jefe was sent to prison, Aurelio banished himself to Los Angeles for a few years, where the brewery owned a house. When he returned to Juárez, he took over the organization he had worked for by killing the man who had informed on his boss. He also killed the man's wife, parents, and children."

Berg picked up the humidor, opened it, and held it out to

me. I declined. He selected a cigar, clipped it, and lit it, puffing it into life.

"Aurelio must be nearly eighty by now and he wears the mask of respectability," Berg said, "but it's common knowledge that the Blancas cartel is one of the biggest in Chihuahua State. The fox may lose its teeth, but not its nature."

"You think these people are behind what's happened to Clay?"

"I'm saying the Blancas connection makes your husband's innocence a certitude."

"I don't understand."

"Señora, if your husband had killed one who the Blancases consider part of their extended family and they knew of it, he would be dead by now. Aurelio Blancas does not wait on someone else for justice."

"Then . . ."

Berg let his head fall back against the chair and angled his gaze at the ceiling, puffing slowly on the Cuban cigar until he was wreathed in smoke. Finally, he sat up and looked across the desk into my eyes.

"There's something else going on here."

"But what?"

"I don't know, but there's something." He paused, turned away. The minutes slipped by. He gave a heavy sigh, again turned his big soft eyes to mine. "What does your husband have that they might want?"

TWENTY-FIVE

Before I left Chihuahua at noon, Tito Berg arranged to communicate with me through Enrique Vera. He relied on his cell phone over unreliable TelMex, but since my area is blocked by the mountains, he couldn't telephone me directly.

Enrique would run any messages to me on the Wednesdays and Sundays that I visited Clay, or, if urgent, he would telephone a message to Dennis Bustamante in Presidio for relay to me.

Berg made no promise of when I'd hear from him. "When I have something, you'll know," he said. "My first priority is to get a date for another hearing. Yours should be to try and find out more about Mehendru's relationship with the Blancas family."

After leaving his office, I stopped at a PEMEX station for gasoline and started for home.

I got back to the trading post around six and found Mike

Dodd sitting on the couch watching a Marx Brothers video and feeding a week-old Inca dove with a syringe.

"Where'd you get the nestling?" I asked, setting down my overnight case and going over to have a closer look at the tiny bird.

"A kid who said his name was Bean dropped it off this morning around eight," Mike said. "A raccoon robbed the nest and he managed to save this one."

"Bean is one of the Ramos grandkids," I told him. "He got that nickname after he got a pinto bean stuck up his nose when he was three."

I watched as Mike finished feeding the dove and placed it gently in a nest of paper shavings in a tissue box.

I looked around the room. "You must have locked Phobe up or she'd have tried to eat your patient."

Mike laughed. "She tried. She and Jefe are in the laundry room. I'm glad you're back," he said. "I'm a little worried about Hugger. I went out to his place this morning to check on the mule I treated last Friday. I knocked on the door and got no answer and he wasn't in the barn, so I honked the horn, but he never came. I waited about thirty minutes. I wish he had a telephone; I'd like to know he's okay."

"So would I. You put the nestling in the clinic. I'll let Phobe and Jefe out, then we'll go out there. We'll take both pickups, in case one of us has to go for help."

Mike carried the nestling out. I released Phobe and Jefe, put down some food for the pair, and picked up both sets of keys. Something as simple as a fall and a broken leg can be fatal out here if you're far from help and no one finds you.

Mike followed me, driving Clay's pickup. It was nearly five when we reached Choke Canyon. Our knocking at the house stirred up the mules in the corral, who lined up along the near fence to watch us as I went in the unlocked door. I knew from the dull quality of the silence that Hugger wasn't there, but I went through all four rooms to be sure he wasn't sick or lying dead from a heart attack in one of them. Mike stood in the doorway, less comfortable than I with inspecting someone else's private domain. The living room had a wall of filled bookshelves, a few comfortable, well-used armchairs, and side tables. There were no dirty dishes in the kitchen sink and no signs of a meal interrupted. The first bedroom was as clean as the rest of the house, the bed made up, with the sheets tucked in tight and the blanket folded at the foot. The second bedroom looked less used. The white-tiled bathroom told me nothing. The bath towel on the rod and the hand towel by the pedestal sink were dry.

Back outside, Mike doubled-checked the barn he'd looked in earlier while I tried to soothe the mules. Were they nervy because we were stangers or because they sensed something amiss? Hugger's absence? Monk came to me as if he remembered I'd helped him. I rubbed his neck.

"Where's Hugger gotten to?" I asked him, quite sure he'd tell me if he knew and could talk.

"Not there," Mike said, returning to my side from the barn. "It doesn't look like anything's disturbed or missing."

"Like the house," I said. "Everything neat and clean."

"What now?" Mike asked.

"We'll follow the black-line pipe toward the spring and see if he's up there."

Mike rode with me. It was only a quarter mile before the black lava boulders thrown up eons ago necessitated our going on foot. The aboveground pipe was easy to follow. Around us, the Arizona ash and cottonwood trees grew steadily thicker. The spring at the top of Choke Canyon must be formidable. I saw signs of raccoons, ringtails, porcupines, bobcat, skunks, and one print that might have been a mountain lion in the dirt trail Hugger had worn. I could see boot marks where someone had walked, but I'm no tracker and they didn't tell me whom they belonged to nor how old they were.

The pipeline took a sudden hook to the right and disappeared behind rock and scrubs. I picked it up several feet farther along, but I didn't need it to find the spring. The circular pool was perhaps twenty feet across, its surface darkened by the shade of overhanging willows. It was backed by a greenish blue grotto, a shallow cave of solid rock that rose a hundred feet.

"What a beautiful place." Mike's silibant whisper echoed into the silence.

"It's a ciénaga," I said.

"What's that?"

"It's Spanish for a spring-fed reservoir."

Mike pointed into the pool. "I meant that."

Deep below in the clear water, shinning in the refracted light, were the exposed red roots of the willows. Hugger Baines lay on his back, tangled among them.

TWENTY-SIX

Thursday, May 2

He was dead when he hit the water, shot in the head right there, with his back to the pool," Dennis Bustamante said. "The Border Patrol tracker found a couple of good shoe prints that weren't his. If we had something to match them to, we might know who killed him."

It was 5:30 A.M., the time of early morning when the wind is stilled for a few hours. The deputy, Mike Dodd, and I sat at the kitchen table, with a pot of coffee and the dirty plates left over from the bacon-and-egg sandwiches I'd prepared. The sheriff and the Border Patrol tracker were still at the murder site, waiting for good light to look for further evidence.

After finding Hugger, Mike and I had driven back to the trading post to telephone the sheriff's office, then Mike had gone to his room to nap, he said, between the nestling dove's feedings. I'd fallen asleep on the couch in my clothes. I woke at 3:00 A.M. with a heavy weight covering me. It was Phobe, stretched out from my neck to my knees. Jefe warmed my feet. I'd put the first pot of coffee on then. Mike came in shortly after I turned on the lights. Dennis Bustamante had arrived an hour later to tell us that Hugger's body was on the way to San Antonio for autopsy.

"Who's going to take care of the mules?" Mike asked.

"We'll arrange for one of the ranches to take them, temporarily," Dennis told him, "until we find out who they belong to now. I never heard Mr. Baines mention any kinfolks."

"Hugger's real name was Canfield," I said, "if that's any help."

"It sure will be," Dennis said, getting to his feet. "Thanks for the breakfast. Can you cut on the pumps for me? I need a fill-up."

"Let us know if you find out anything about who killed Hugger" I said, letting Dennis out the front door. I turned on the pumps and took the ticket book outside for him to sign. When I got back to the kitchen, Mike was washing the dishes.

"I only just met Hugger, but I liked him," Mike said, setting the last cup to drain. "I can't believe he's dead. What reason could anyone have for killing him?"

"I don't know," I said, getting out the food bowls for Phobe and Jefe. Mike sat down at the table while I cut up Phobe's food log. I put the bowls down and Phobe and Jefe emptied them almost instantly. "He had a good life up there in the canyon."

"You seemed surprised the spring was there," Mike said.

I explained that Hugger had mentioned a spring, but out here that could mean a mud hole with a trickle of water oozing out of it. "I doubt that many people knew about the ciénaga. Hugger kept to himself, and so did the previous owner. Old Pedro Tampaleo owned the place most of my life. He came here from a village below Juárez when he was just a boy and worked as a cowhand on the ranches. The last people he worked for, a couple named Halters, owned the Double Bar.

Choke Canyon was part of that ranch. Mrs. Halters died first, then her husband about three months later. They left Choke Canyon to Pedro and he lived on it the better part of forty years. He was nearly ninety when he sold it to Hugger. He used to bring me persimmons, little bitty ones, full of seed, but so sweet. No wonder Bonis Avidus tried to buy Choke Canyon from Hugger. I wonder how they knew about the ciénaga?"

"Probably aerial photography."

"You know about this?" I asked.

"My brother's degree is in environmental biology. He's flown with some of the groups when they grid off an area for a photo fly-over. They use the information to partially determine environmental damage and wildlife numbers."

It was also one way to find out about land without asking the owner. "From the air that ciénaga would stand out like a business suit at a barbecue," I said, mostly to myself.

"It's an astonishing place," Mike said. "This whole country is. I've never been anywhere so empty, so far from lights. I never appreciated real darkness before. It's like a whole different world out here."

I smiled at him. He was a good veterinarian and a good person. And he had a bad case of Trans-Pecos-itis, a disease we locals see a lot of. The bigger the city that first-time visitors come from, the worse the case. They fall in love with the landscape, the romance of living the ranching life, being a "cowboy." They buy the hat, the shirt, the jeans, and the boots. They buy the ranch, the cows, and hire a "ranch manager," even if the ranch is only a couple of hundred acres. They become instant experts on everything rural and bovine. Maybe a third stay on. The rest go on to the next place they think will be the one that will change them into something they aren't and don't really want to be. Mike, I thought, might be genuine, a stayer.

"Time for me to feed Squib again," he said.

"You named the nestling?"

"I couldn't resist. See you later."

The rest of the day was more or less normal. Mike had only one client, who brought in a sweet little mutt and left him overnight to be neutered. I had a number of customers, some of whom had already heard about the murder of Hugger Baines and were eager to talk.

After dinner Mike, looking as if finding Hugger had caught up to him, went straight to the guest room. I took a whiskey out to the porch and watched the remains of the day melt into shadow. Three or four lazy buzzards wheeled slowly in the last rays of the sun, two quail chattered to each other as they moved toward the river in search of water, a white-winged dove fluttered into the trees to settle for the night. As the tops of the mountains turned golden red, I caught sight of the first of the nighthawks making passes above the trees. Then came the bats, silhouetted against the gray-blue sky. And somewhere, out in the center of the river, some predator splashed vainly in the few pools where once, before the drought, there would have been fish for raccoons and coyotes to catch.

Water, water everywhere, and not a drop to drink. The line of poetry came unbidden, a memory from my school days. But it referred to an ocean, not a desert where there wasn't a drop, except rarely. Like the ciénaga, which had drawn coyotes and cougars, mice and jackrabbits. And among them, two humans: one a predator, the other the prey.

TWENTY-SEVEN

Friday, May 3

I had to make a trip to Marfa. Mike volunteered to sit in for me at the trading-post counter.

"As long as I'm feeding Squib every thirty minutes, I may as well be doing something else useful. If I have to go out on a call, I'll close up," he said.

After breakfast, Mike went back to the guest room to get Squib, the nestling, in its tissue box. We hid the tiny gray-buff bird from Phobe's abundant curiosity for all things feathered and eatable by putting it in the deep drawer under the counter. Not that she wouldn't know it was there—her sense of smell would tell her that—but she couldn't open the drawer.

I was showing Mike the list of video rentals when the angry yowl came from beneath the counter.

Phobe had gone under the counter and tried to come at Squib from the back. One big front paw was firmly wedged in the narrow space between the drawer and the underside of the counter. Phobe hung there, her weight resting on her haunches, unable to pull free, squirming in frustration.

I lay on my back, the top half of my body under the counter space with Phobe. I held her trapped leg with one hand, wrapped my other arm firmly around her middle so she couldn't move suddenly and hurt herself. "Open the drawer slowly," I told Mike. As he did, I lifted her slightly and held her paw flat, straightening her leg as the drawer moved until she was free. "Get Squib," I said, afraid to release Phobe until Mike had the nestling in hand.

"Got her," he said. I released Phobe. She walked past man and bird, giving a hiss of disapproval.

Rescue over, I changed into a lemon-colored shirtwaist dress and flat-heeled shoes and by ten was cruising at seventy-five miles per hour on Highway 67 north to Marfa.

The county seat has changed over the past few years. Renovation has given the old adobe and stucco buildings a face-lift and there are more in-comers living in town. A few live there full-time, but many are part-timers whose commitment to the community might or might not prove to be for the long-term good. The locals who were making money from the modest surge in the town's commerce embrace the changes. I admire Marfa's new look; I'm not sure about her new persona.

A smiling man on a blue racing bike banked around a corner as I turned off Highland Avenue onto Quero Street. One of the people I didn't know, but he waved like an old friend and I waved back.

Eileen Washington's office was tucked into the corner of her family's furniture store on the corner across from Saint Mary's Catholic Church. I pulled into the head-on parking, pleased to see Eileen's gold Buick parked nearby. The real estate agent was in.

Eileen was on the telephone. She waved me to a chair by her overflowing desk. I moved a stack of real estate forms to the floor and sat down.

"No, the buyer will be in Santa Fe that day," Eileen was saying as she doodled on a notepad in front of her, "but that's not a problem. I'll fax him the contracts." She spun in her chair and circled a calendar date in red, chirped "Bye," and hung up, turning to squeeze my hand.

"I've been meaning to call you," she said. "It's terrible what's happened to Clay. How is he? How are you?"

I've known Eileen since I was thirteen. Through junior high and high school, we'd competed against each other in basketball and shared an empathetic understanding of being the two tallest girls on teams of otherwise skimpy five-foot-fivers.

"We're doing okay," I told her. "We're waiting on the new hearing date to be set. I'm here to talk with you about selling my land."

"The trading post?"

"I'm keeping it and forty acres."

"So the rest of the section, six hundred acres."

"Yes. The sooner you can sell it, the better."

"We have people from Houston, Dallas, New York, and even Santa Fe looking for small acreage. I think I know someone who'll be interested. Did you have a price in mind?"

"What do you recommend?" I said, wishing that when I'd had the chance, I'd asked Hugger how much Bonis Avidus had offered for Choke Canyon, so I'd have something to go on. Neither Eileen nor the only other real estate agent in the county ran prices in their newspaper ads. I know, because I'd looked after I made up my mind to sell.

"Any proven water?" Eileen asked.

"A well, but it goes with the trading post."

"Any improvements?"

"No."

As to confirm where my land was located, she glanced up at the three-foot-square map of Presidio County mounted on the wall next to her desk. The big ranch headquarters, Polvo, even the trading post, were identified. Small holdings were grouped together and marked simply "Various Owners."

Wells were marked with a circle and the word "Water" in bold-face type. I had the same map displayed on the north wall of the trading post.

"You might think about having a well drilled on the parcel you're selling," she said. "We can add the cost to the price, so you won't be out anything and it would help sell it."

Giving myself time to think, I got up to look at the map. It was old, printed about the time I was in college and never updated since, but Eileen had marked every new land ownership change, including the newly subdivided Jackson Ranch.

"I didn't realize so much property had changed hands," I said.

"Yes, especially recently," Eileen said. "It's been very busy around here and several of the big ranches in your area have sold. I haven't marked them because I didn't handle the sales, so I don't yet know who the new owners are. I've been meaning to ask at the title company, but I'm always thinking of my own business when I'm there."

"I hadn't heard about any sales," I said.

"The Motts sold out, which wasn't unexpected, given their age. Though I'd have thought some of the children would want to keep it in the family. What surprised me was Bill Picket selling. I thought he loved it out here."

"Maybe someone offered so much he couldn't say no," I said. "Did you handle any of the sales of the Jackson land after Bonis Avidus carved it up?"

Eileen rolled her eyes. "I had a client who wanted to buy the headquarters. I'd been working with them for months and nothing suited until they saw that. I called that woman who runs Bonis Avidus, Christiana Jacobs. She said how much she appreciated the referral. It wasn't until after she took my client's name and telephone number that she informed me that the by-laws of the organization didn't allow, as she put it, for 'contractual obligations with real estate agents.' "

"She wouldn't pay your fee?" I said.

"Not a penny. I told her I wasn't a charity, nor was I tax-free like her group, and that my clients would find something elsewhere, if I had anything to say about it. She doesn't work for nothing, I'll bet," Eileen said bitterly. "I checked around. Bonis Avidus is tight fisted when it comes to laying out cash. They buy land occasionally, but only when they can get it at below market value, like the Jackson ranch. Mostly they get owners to donate what they call 'environmental corridors' on their land, slices of the place that are easements in perpetuity."

"So neither the owner nor the heirs can sell?"

"Right, but they still foot the property tax bill, and that's only part of it. Bonis expects—"

The telephone on the desk rang. Eileen leaned over and checked caller ID. "I need to take this," she said to me, picking up. She then asked the caller to hold, placed her hand over the receiver and said, "Why don't you run across the street to the water board's office and talk to Mack Friedel. Maybe he can tell you the odds of hitting water if you drill."

I nodded and left. I could see the posted sign, TRI-COUNTY WATER PLANNING BOARD, in the front window of the rented office on the corner opposite the church. The board, a group of twelve appointed citizens from among the three counties represented—Presidio, Brewster, and Jeff Davis—had the unenviable, state-mandated task of figuring out how, in our desert region, we were to manage our water supply in the projected very dry future and how that water would be divided among rural and city interests. It was the object of much derision on the part of locals because generations of experience had taught us that it was almost impossible to predict where groundwater might be located.

The board had until fall to present a fifty-year use plan to the Texas Water Development Board. In the fourteen months since the local board had been formed, the members had argued endlessly over minute details like the wording of their policy statement, and accomplished only one practical objective, the hiring of a consultant to study where and in what quantities water might be found. Most of us considered the board useless and paid little attention to them. I didn't know the members' names, and in that I probably was typical, but if Eileen thought the board might have information that would be helpful, I was willing to ask.

I waited while the one pickup on the street passed, then crossed and went into the office. The walls of the square room were covered in maps of the tri-county region.

Mack Friedel, a round man with a magnanimous smile, looked up from some charts and graphs spread over the wide desk and greeted me.

"What can you tell me about the groundwater here?" I said, pointing to the appropriate dot on the Presidio County map. "I'm selling some land and a live well would help."

"Water's a plus, all right," Mack said, getting to his feet and coming from behind the desk to stand by the map. "Using existing wells and known springs is one way to determine available but unknown and untapped underground water resources. You're well within this zone." He drew his finger along an imaginary line that connected the widespread wells like mine along the river to those on the big ranches that encircled us.

"Is that good?" I asked.

"You know what oilman T. Boone Pickens says? 'Water is going to be the oil of the future.'"

"So you think there's groundwater to be found under my section?"

"I think so," he said, "but I can't say more than that, you understand, until the board makes the hydrologist's finding public. There is still work to be done before we do that."

"You sound confident," I said.

He smiled, looking pleased with himself. "Take one of our cards," he said, reaching for one from the stack on the desk. "In case you have questions later."

I walked back to Eileen's office.

"Any luck?" she said.

"Nothing definite. Let's price the land without a well and see what happens," I said, recalling the difficulty and expense some of my far-flung neighbors had had in hitting water. It took drilling a couple of test wells before you struck water. I'd known people to call in water witchers in an attempt to fix a likely spot to drill after three or four test wells came up as dry as their pocketbooks. I had too much on my mind to go out of my way to add another worry.

"You're selling at the right time," Eileen said. "Everyone is looking for something away from the city."

"I'm away, that's for sure."

"On the raw land, let's start at five hundred an acre," she said. "You can always come down if you have to."

I did the math. "Three hundred thousand dollars."

"You could get more if you divided it into three parcels."

"No, no, three hundred thousand will do," I said, my heart fluttering in relief. Not dividing the land allowed Clay and me to retain more privacy and still provided a built-in cushion to cover the expenses Berg had mentioned. I signed the one-page agreement making Eileen my agent and left feeling for the first time since Clay's arrest that I'd accomplished something purposeful in aid of him.

I got home as darkness claimed the landscape. Round-trip, I'd driven two hundred and and twenty-five miles, I'd been gone six hours, forty-one minutes, and used a tank of gas.

"It wasn't until I emptied my pockets before hanging up my dress that I looked at the card Mack Friedel had given me. Zanjiv Mehendru's name appeared in tiny print as one of the twelve members of the Tri-County Water Planning Board.

TWENTY-EIGHT

Sunday, May 5

The wind had died down around 4:00 A.M. and hadn't returned, a sure sign spring was vanquished. Summer in the desert arrives not on any official calendar date, but on the first day the temperature hits one hundred degrees. We'd been hovering at ninety-nine degrees for days.

On Saturday, Claudia had brought over freshly cooked brisket with Ruben's Habanero sauce. I wrapped slices of it in foil along with onions, hard-boiled eggs, and a loaf of bread, and left to spend my two hours with Clay. On the way, as had become my habit, I tuned in to Radio Ojinaga.

"Clean up the system," the morning talk-show host shouted. "Why has Magistrado Resendez ignored proof offered by Chief of Police Santo Girón that the prosecution's eyewitness, Aida Machuca, was incarcerated on the night of the murder? What pressures were brought on this woman, a known drug addict, to lie? Why has Aida Machuca disappeared from the streets of Ojinaga? Are we to believe what the authorities tell us? That she's in a drug rehabilitation center going through withdrawal? Why won't the magistrado or the prosecutor answer the media's questions? What are they hiding? It's corruption of the legal system. I think the magistrado is afraid he'll be fired. I think the prosecutor wants to clear a case more than he wants to find the real killer. I think fronterizo Clay Jones is a scapegoat. What do you think, Ojinaga?"

I felt elation and dismay. It's good to know that others are on your side, but it's scary to have your life gone so wrong that it's the subject of a talk show.

Surprise gave way to more surprise after I crossed the bridge and entered Ojinaga and saw JUSTICE FOR JONES written in white shoe polish on the rear window of a car. The first shop window I passed had a poster: FREE CLAY JONES. As I drove, I saw another, and another, and another.

In front of the prison, about thirty people carrying placards moved in a slow circle in the street chanting, "Freedom for Jones, Freedom for Jones." As I got out of the pickup, Olivia Berrera separated herself from the mix of demonstrators, vendors, and prison visitors and hurried to meet me, smiling and looking pleased with herself.

"You see the support your husband gets! Our demonstrations will pressure the authorities," she said, embracing me with her free arm. With the other, she held up the placard so I could see the printed slogan: JUSTICE HAS NO COUNTRY. IT BELONGS TO ALL. FREE THE NORTÉAMERICANO.

"You arranged all this?" I said.

"Radio Ojinaga arranged this after my guest appearance on the "Juan Lara Show.""

Juan Lara was the talk-show host I'd just been listening to on the radio.

"I was on Friday morning. Juan has taken up Clay's cause," Olivia said. "Isn't it wonderful?"

"Wonderful," I said. In my heart, I hoped all the publicity wouldn't so anger the magistrate and the prosecutor and the judiciales that they'd dig in their heels.

"Between Juan Lara and the editorials on Clay's behalf in *La Voz de Ojinaga,* the authorities will be embarrassed into doing what's right," Olivia said.

I left Olivia chanting with her fellow protesters. The gatekeeper let me in and I walked to Clay's cell. He sat on his cot, leaning against the stained and pockmarked wall, the bottle of Lysol open on the crate beside him to mask the prison odor that hung in the hot air.

Clay knew about the demonstrators. "The other prisoners like it," he said. "It breaks up the day. They stand at the gate and watch and beg cigarettes."

"Are you okay with it?" I said, knowing he'd find the notoriety distasteful. I wanted him to talk, complain, react. I didn't like the grayness of his skin and the apparent weight loss.

"I resent my life being made over into someone else's cause," he said. "Funny how a personal tragedy becomes a public forum, how other people assume you welcome their interference at any price."

"I understand and I agree, but we can't pick and choose who supports us and how," I said. "Not now."

"I much prefer Jack's prayers to public parades."

"I understand how you feel," I said, getting out the food, setting the Lysol on the floor so I could use the crate for a table. Clay ate little of his lunch, blaming the heat for his lack of appetite, but it was the helplessness of having his fate in the hands of others that was the cause of his malaise.

I repacked the food in the cooler and, seeking relief from the close air, we walked around the compound, following in the same tight circle as many of the other families.

"Like Sunday on the plaza," I said, trying to earn a smile from Clay.

We walked, not touching because it was too hot. Finally, I brought up the subject I'd dreaded.

"I've put six hundred acres up for sale," I said. "The money will more than take care of the lawyer's fee."

"How much will that be?" Clay said. He stopped still when I told him Berg's fee. "I hate that I'm costing you your land," he said.

"I'd hate it more if we didn't have the land to sell." I put my arm through Clay's and started us moving again. Telling him about Hugger's death was harder than I'd imagined.

We both felt the loss of a man of such decency. "What possible reason could anyone have to kill Hugger?" Clay said.

We stopped in a corner and watched the other prisoners and their families, people whom we now knew by name, who greeted us as friends because we shared a common experience, because this world was more real than the outside to those who couldn't leave it. My visits were making it harder, not easier, for Clay. Day by day, he adjusted to a life thrust on him, forgetting himself in using his veterinary skills even under such circumstances. Then I came along and reminded him of all from which he was separated, all that he might lose for a long time to come. I saw the same emotional conflict in the faces of the other prisoners when they looked at their wives and children, their expressions a mix of love tinged with dread. It made life in El Cereso that much harder.

When the guard called time, instead of walking me to the gate as he usually did, Clay said good-bye at the door of his cell and went and sat on the cot. Walking away, I forced myself not to look back, not wanting Clay to see my anxiety. At the gate, one of the guards, a tall man with reflector sunglasses hiding his eyes, approached me.

"Warden Martinez would like to see you, señora."

As the guard ushered me into the office, the warden leaped up from behind the desk. "I have Señor's Clay's share of the pesos from our little business," he said, as the guard was closing the door. In the corner of the room, his old father sat nodding in his wheelchair, Zapata the cat curled up on his lap, watching me attentively.

"How is your father today?" I asked.

"Better than he seems," the warden said. "Please, sit down, Señora Jones. We must talk."

"About the money?"

"That was for the benefit of the guard." The warden leaned against the edge of the desk and spoke in a conspiratorial whisper. "Someone is watching Señor Clay."

"Watching?"

"Another prisoner. A man named Manuel Rivera, in the next cell. He's been observed taking note of who comes to see Señor Clay and when. He reports this information to his wife, when she comes to visit him. She also comes with questions about Señor Clay. Is he sleeping badly? Is he eating? Is he getting worried about what is going to happen to him? In conversations with your husband, the prisoner has been saying how innocent men go to prison while the guilty ones buy their freedom with bribes."

"Why would he do such a thing?" I said.

"Señora, I do not know, except that someone must be paying him, because suddenly he has money for cigarettes and other things, when before all he had was what his wife could supply, and she is without work and has four little ones at home to care for." The warden bent close. "Listen to me. Everyone knows this case against Señor Clay is a fraud. Aida Machuca hasn't been seen in Ojinaga since the first hearing. Talk on the street is that the judiciales have her in custody in a private drug rehabilitation center in Chihuahua City. I ask myself, Why? Such places are for the rich. Someone must be paying, and it isn't the judiciales."

"How did you find out about this Rivera?" I asked.

The warden straightened and smiled. I followed his gaze in the direction of his old father, who no longer nodded listlessly, but sat watching me intently, his eyes bright with intelligence. He winked.

My father was a bus driver until he lost the use of his legs in a crash," the warden said. "He was bored at home, so I said he could help me here. One can never know enough about what goes on in the prison, so he sits in his wheelchair and looks blank or pretends to doze. The prisoners are so used to seeing him, they forget he's there. Already, his big ears have helped me to prevent several little problems from developing into big headaches." The warden stood up and circled to the door. "You should go now, or it will seem suspicious that we take so long. "He grasped the doorknob. "On your next visit, you will warn Señor Clay to be circumspect in his future conversation with Rivera?"

"I will, but perhaps you should talk with him."

The warden shook his head. "The less I'm seen talking privately with Señor Clay, the better. The people who are paying Rivera might notice and approach me. A poor man can withstand only so much temptation."

TWENTY-NINE

I took advantage of being in Ojinaga to see Mercedes Solar.

She welcomed me as if I'd been expected. I'd come more than half in anger, thinking she'd betrayed me by not revealing Mehendru's connection to the Blancas family, but standing in her presence, I remembered her essential kindness, the gentleness she'd shown in talking with me in the first place.

"You've seen the signs around town, I'm sure, in support of your husband," she said as we went to sit at the table under the desert willow. The soft shade reduced the temperature, making it almost pleasant. She poured me a glass of water from the pitcher on the table.

"It's gratifying," I said. "I just hope it won't hurt Clay more than it helps."

"Likely it won't do either. If it's sloppy work by the judiciales and a prosecutor who's willing to railroad an innocent man in order to make a name for himself, a little local public opposition won't count for much. If it's something more, if it goes higher, then it counts even less."

"So I shouldn't be comforted or concerned," I said.

"So often we think we can make a difference, when really we have next to no effect beyond the shouting," she said sadly, then caught her own negative tone and shook her head as if to clear it. "Forgive me. That sounds so like something Zanjiv might have said."

"Don't apologize. I had the same thought when I saw the demonstrators," I told her. "My friend Olivia would say that it's the trying that helps. Maybe she's right. It did lift my spirits, seeing those posters."

"Then it's good," she said. Before, she had looked fragile; today she looked almost frail. There were shadows beneath her eyes and her shoulders slumped in defeat. Her physical deterioration might be delayed shock and grief at her lover's death; or had some fresh blow, coupled with the first, so devastated her?

"I don't want to intrude on your privacy, but sometimes it helps to talk," I said.

She looked around her at the garden and drew a deep breath. "Zanjiv bought this house for me. He said it was to be my security. I loved it. I thought, no matter what, I can manage because I have a place to come to, a home of my own, a refuge." She looked down at her hands in her lap. "After he was killed, my anger at whoever did this to him kept me going. I seem to have run out of anger. This house is nothing. It means nothing. It gives me nothing. Zanjiv was my refuge."

The tears in her eyes spilled over and rolled down her face. Shortly, she calmed herself and went to wash her face.

"Someday," she said, when she returned, "you and I must talk when things are happy for both of us."

We sat quietly for a while. I watched a pair of wrens flitting to the ground and back to a nest in a hanging basket of red geraniums.

"You asked me to speak to Daniel," I said when I thought

enough time had passed for her to be less vulnerable to her emotions. "I asked a close friend of his to tell him that you wanted to see him."

"That was good of you. I thought Daniel might want to talk with someone else who loved his father. I thought he might need someone, not having any other family. I was wrong. He isn't alone. He has a lawyer," she said dryly. "It seems that Zanjiv bequeathed one half of his estate to me. A lawyer representing Daniel wrote to me, informing me of this and requesting me to sign a document renouncing any interest in the estate. If I fail to sign, the letter informed me, not only will Daniel Mehendru contest the will, he will take this house, too." She paused. "I never wanted Zanjiv's money, but I resent threats."

"I doubt that Daniel can take the house. As for your interest in the estate, I think you should go to Marfa and hire a lawyer," I told her. "Fight it. Zanjiv wanted you to have the money."

"I wish he hadn't. I told him, when I accepted the house, that it was the only thing I would take from him."

"He must have had his reasons."

She looked up at me with such sadness in her expression. "Yes. Poor Zanjiv. Still trying to make it up to me." *

She spoke the last words to herself. After a while, she straightened in her chair, came back from whatever memory she had slipped away to. "You've been more help than you know," she said. "I've done nothing but indulge my emotions since you arrived, but you must have come here for a purpose."

"To ask a question. What was Zanjiv's relationship with his stepfather, Aurelio Blancas?"

"How did you know about that?" she asked.

I explained about the *El Diario* news article I'd read while in Chihuahua.

"I can't imagine how the reporter got that information," she said, a small frown creasing her brow.

"Are you saying Mehendru's connection to the Blancas family wasn't generally known?"

"Zanjiv would never have told anyone," she said. "It was his secret, but the need to keep it died with him. I think I told you that my father was a custom broker in Juárez."

"You did."

"He made a good living. We weren't rich, but we were secure. We had a nice house. My brother Alecio was going to start college in the fall, and my father had just bought him a new car. One day, in July, my father came home early from his office. He called my mother, my brother, and me into his office. He told us that he'd been approached by Aurelio Blancas and offered the gold or the lead." Mercedes looked me in the eye. "Do you know what that means?"

"The money or the bullet."

"Yes. Aurelio Blancas wanted to use my father's business to smuggle drugs across the border. He would select the cargo, bring in the shipments, provide false documents in the names of companies that didn't exist. All my father had to do was turn his back and carry on as usual. For this, he'd be well paid," Mercedes said bitterly. "All he had to risk was his livelihood and going to jail if a shipment was discovered at the border."

"He refused?"

"Yes. My mother begged him to move, to go somewhere else. My father said such men were everywhere and he wouldn't give in to a man like Blancas. He said he'd take every precaution, hire a bodyguard and guards for the office. I think he believed in his heart that when it came to it, Aurelio would back down. Our families were close. We'd been in each other's homes, Zanjiv and Alecio were best friends, my mother hoped I'd marry Zanjiv."

She touched her hand to her mouth. I knew what was coming, knew this was the event that had shaped the future of two families.

"A month later, my father and brother were gunned down in front of a restaurant. Alecio lived for two days. Zanjiv came to the hospital to see him. He didn't know, you see, until my mother screamed it at him in the corridor—that his stepfather was a drug dealer and a murderer. Afterward, my mother forbade me to see Zanjiv. But I did, once. He came one night and tapped on my window, I climbed out and we sat on the roof and talked. He'd tried to tell his mother what kind of man Aurelio was. He wanted her to leave him. She refused to believe the truth. Or didn't want to. She liked her luxuries and Aurelio provided them. Zanjiv had already won a full scholarship to the University of Texas. He left for Austin that night. He never forgave his mother, nor she him. She died six months ago. I saw her obituary in the newspaper. Zanjiv's name wasn't listed as one of the survivors, only her three children by Aurelio."

"What about Aurelio?" I asked. "How did he feel?"

"If the Blancases thought about Zanjiv at all, which is doubtful, it wouldn't be with kindness. Aurelio was nothing if not proud. And Zanjiv had nothing but contempt for his stepfather. He wanted nothing to do with him, or his mother, after she chose her second family over him. More important, he never wanted such people in his son's life," she added with finality. "He told Daniel his grandparents were dead."

"And Mehendru's mother never tried to get in touch with him? Even after his move back to El Paso as head of the Boundary Commission?"

"Never," Solar said. " 'Our lives are the result of our choices,' that's what Zanjiv used to say. His mother had made her choice and he had made his. He never looked back."

Solar walked me to the gate. She'd given me answers that had only led to more questions neither of us could answer.

Then who had told *El Diario* about the connection? How

had the Blancases' names come to be listed in Mehendru's obituary in the *International?* Why was Kimberly Blancas de Gaza, according to Crosse, staying with Daniel at the ranch? It was time for me to pay a visit to the next of kin.

THIRTY

Thursday, May 9

For three days in succession, I had tried to reach Daniel Mehendru on the telephone, but the answering machine always picked up. I left one message, but Daniel hadn't returned the call. Finally, I decided to go in person and hope that Daniel would talk with me if we were face-to-face. Mike had to be out TB-testing a herd, so I put up the CLOSED sign, then started for the Sloe Ranch.

Beyond Polvo, the road runs out, becoming a lava-rock track that washes out whenever there is a drop or two of rain. In dry weather, only four-wheel-drive vehicles can negotiate the deep ruts. Here the ancient lava flows spread out in fans. The track rides these as far as one can drive along the lonely passage. At mile six, I crossed a dry slough, turning north and then west along a ranch road that ran in an irregular route as it climbed under an incredible blue sky toward the rimrock.

The Sloe Ranch is approached through another, larger holding marked only by a cattle guard. A wooden sign with the name burned on like a brand denoted the entrance to the two- thousand-acre Mehendru property, a hobby ranch in our area.

Beyond the entrance, the road had been graveled. I could see a white house glimmering at the end of the long drive. Up close, the stuccoed building with a columned portico still had that new look. There were no cattle in the pastures and, as I parked in front of the house, no dogs came running to greet the pickup and no one came out to identify their visitor.

I crossed the porch and knocked on the door. Silence. I sat in one of the rattan chairs grouped under the portico and waited. Twenty minutes later, I heard the sound of a smooth motor. A white Suburban came slowly up the drive and parked behind my pickup. I stood up and walked to the porch edge.

Daniel Mehendru, in a navy shirt and khaki slacks, got out on the passenger side, saw me, and nervously flicked back a curl of hair that had fallen over his forehead. He looked caught between surprise and distaste at my presence and stopped where he was, turning around to look back at the woman who'd been driving as she walked around the vehicle. Designer sunglasses hid her eyes. Black hair was cut so that it tucked in around her jawline, framing a square face. Her red lipstick and glossy polish were the exact color of her pantsuit.

"Daniel," I said, trying to be vague and polite about my being there, "I've been wanting to see you. I'd have come sooner, but for the circumstances. Now that the newspapers have made it clear to the public that there's no evidence linking my husband with your father's death, I felt we could talk." Daniel smiled, but his eyes were cold.

His good manners saved me. He turned to the woman standing next to him and said, "Aunt Kim, this is Mrs. Jones."

"Kim Blancas de Garza," she said, removing the sunglasses and looking at me with heavily made-up brown eyes. I guessed her age at early forties.

"Texana, please," I said.

"I've read the newspaper accounts of your husband's arrest and detention. One always wonders if such stories are accurate," she said.

"I can vouch for the fact that my husband was on an emergency call and then at home with me on the night of the murder," I said quietly.

"Well, you've had a long drive. Come in and have something cool to drink." She slipped past me.

Daniel gave me a searching look with wary eyes, and followed her into the house.

The front door opened directly into a carpeted living room that went through to double French doors opening onto another portico. At one end of the wide room, two leather couches faced each other in front of a stone fireplace. The tables were all glass-topped with iron legs. The comfortable chairs at the other side of the room were grouped around a low table with neat stacks of magazines. Curtains, carpet, and upholstery were in natural tones, browns and greens, with black accents. The furnishings had been selected for comfort rather than style. There was no clutter to gather dust, no pictures or vases or artwork, but plenty of comfortable seating and lamps for reading. No television, but a Bose CD player and a big collection of CDs. Clearly Zanjiv Mehendru had intended this as a retreat, a quiet place to enjoy the retirement that would have come soon enough had he lived.

Kim Garza invited me to sit down, said she'd get us iced coffee from the refrigerator, and left the room. Daniel perched on one couch, looking uncomfortable.

"What a lovely room," I said. Prowling around as if looking at it, I made my way to an open door, through which I could see a desk, computer, and file cabinets. "Was this your father's office?"

"Yes."

"I guess he brought work home, too."

"He was always busy," Daniel said.

"I'm glad you have your aunt with you. I didn't know you had family other than your father," I lied, since Crosse had told me about "Aunt Kim." I doubted that he'd mentioned to Daniel he'd passed that detail on to me.

"Aunt Kim came as soon as she heard," Daniel said. "She's been great. They all have."

I went to sit on the couch opposite Daniel. "All?"

"My uncles and my grandfather and cousins," he said.

"I had no idea you had such a large family."

"Neither did I," Daniel said. "If my grandmother hadn't sent for me, I'd never have found out about them."

As Daniel spoke, Kim Garza returned with a tray and three glasses. She set the tray on the table, handed me a glass in which milky ice floated in brownish black coffee, then went to sit by her nephew, putting one of her well-manicured hands on his knee. To calm him or quiet him? I didn't know which, but it seemed to work. Daniel leaned back and relaxed.

"Family is important in our culture," Kim Garza said. "We don't desert each other."

"My father deserted Grandmother," Daniel said bitterly. "She told me so."

"That's all in the past," Garza said, leaning close to her nephew and patting his knee. "What's important is that we found you." She looked across the table at me. "My mother was diagnosed with cancer too advanced for any treatment. She wanted to get to know Daniel in the little time she had left. She'd never seen him because my half-brother Zanjiv broke with the family when he was seventeen."

"So Mr. Mehendru reconciled with his mother?"

"We thought it best," Kim Garza said, "not to upset Zanjiv, so Daniel visited with the family during the week, when Zanjiv was at work."

Some family, encouraging a son to lie to his father.

"Mrs. Jones, we are so grateful to you for coming to express your sympathy," Garza said smoothly, "and you have ours. We must hope your trouble soon resolves itself. You'll forgive us, but we have to go out again soon for a social engagement and we must dress." She rose. "I'll walk you out."

I put down my untouched coffee and got up, as relieved to be going as she was to see me out.

I had an hour's drive home and it was getting dark as I went out the ranch gate. Had Zanjiv Mehendru found out that his only child was seeing the Blancas family? Had he told his son the truth about Aurelio Blancas and the break with his mother? Had Daniel ignored it or disbelieved it? Daniel seemed to resent his father in favor of loyalty to the dead grandmother. And that loyalty seemed to include the whole Blancas family. What, if anything, did Daniel's comfortable relationship with his newfound family have to do with Mehendru's murder? At a young age Zanjiv Mehendru had been exposed to the reality of evil. It had made him into a man who had no tolerance for those who stretched the law even minimally. He would have been, I guessed, a strict father. Perhaps too strict, never allowing his only son the freedom to make his own mistakes until the time had come when the single mistake Daniel chose to make was to ally himself with the family his father had been at such pains to protect him from.

I drove with the window down, under the amber glow of a full moon that turned the passing scenery into a surreal landscape of sharp whites, grays, and blacks. The bouncing-ball cry of the little screech owl—el tecolotito—filled the night.

At the trading post, the guest room window was dark. Mike had parked Clay's pickup out front.

I went in the back door. Mike had left a note propped on the counter. He'd taken two messages for me, the first from someone named Edmund Cutler asking me to call and giving a 729 number—Marfa. The name meant nothing to me and I wondered if it had to do with my land for sale. The second message drove the first right out of my mind. Enrique Vera had called to say that Clay had been granted a new hearing, set for June 3.

THIRTY-ONE

Friday, May 10

I left for Ojinaga in time to see Clay for the morning's five-minute visitation period so that I could tell him about the new hearing. The heat rose in waves from the pavement. When I passed the Presidio National Bank, the three-foot-tall thermometer on the side read 103 degrees.

At El Cereso, the line of demonstrators had dwindled from the original numbers down to a persistent few. Only three vendors, all selling frozen paletas on a stick in sharp colors of red, green, and blue, worked the sidewalk.

I was walking with the other visitors through the prison yard toward the cells when a fat guard with a cast in one eye told me I'd find my husband in the municipal courtyard. I passed down the dim office hallway and out the other side. The vetmobile had been pulled under the thin shade of the parched tree. Guards stood at either end, while at the back a straggly line had formed: an old man with a gray donkey on the end of a rope, a barefoot boy in a tattered shirt and shorts cradling a fat brown puppy in his arms, a tired-looking woman holding a yellow cage with a green parrot inside, and a middle-aged man with a brightly plumed rooster tucked under one arm. Inside the van, Clay was examining a trembling dog on the fold-down table while its owner leaned in the open doors.

I stood and watched my husband do the thing he loved most in the world, practice his profession. Warden Martinez appeared in the doorway, waved to me, and came over.

"He enjoys his work, no?" the warden said.

"He loves it," I said. "I came to tell him his new lawyer got a hearing date for the first week of June."

"This is good," he said. "Tito Berg is known even here in Ojinaga as a person of importance. No doubt he will prevail and your husband's incarceration will come to an end. On the other matter we talked of, my father tells me the man Rivera continues to watch and inform."

"I told Clay what you said about the man. He's being careful, but he thought it would be too obvious if he stopped talking to him altogether."

"That's wise," the warden said. "If there's one thing I've learned in this business, it's that there's treachery everywhere."

Clay caught sight of me and motioned me over. I told him about the hearing while he gave the puppy an antibiotic shot and counted out pills for the owner to take with him. He didn't react.

"Clay, you do understand what this means, don't you?"

He looked at me with such resignation in his eyes that I regretted having come to tell him. "What good will another hearing do when the result is inevitable?" He handed the puppy's owner the plastic bottle of pills and told him when and how to give them to the animal. I turned and walked away.

After I left the prison and had crossed the bridge, I was held up at O'Reilly by a long line of pickups heading southeast. I looked in the direction they were going and saw a staked notice reading JACKSON FARMS LIQUIDATION SALE and a red arrow. Instead of turning for home, I went with the traffic.

Several dozen vehicles, some hauling empty flatbeds, had parked along the Ranch Road 170 adjacent to Jackson Farms. Four tour buses marked CHARTER were parked by the gates.

I drove past, found an empty spot at the end of the line, and parked. Just inside the gate, a man wearing a hat with "Valley Grower's Association" on it held out a flyer.

"We hope you'll support us."

I glanced at the heading: FARMERS & CAMPESINOS BLOCK-ADE FOR WATER RIGHTS. I waited until I was a few feet away before stuffing it in my pocket. Inside the fenced compound, men in straw hats, thick work shirts, jeans, and work boots congregated on the flat open dirt terrace where heavy farm equipment had been parked in a line, each bearing a numbered tag. The door of the brick office building was open. I passed the men walking around the equipment, no doubt assessing its value in their heads, and went inside. Everything from tables to trash baskets was tagged.

True stood talking on the telephone. His desk was marked for sale at forty dollars, the brass desk lamp at thirty.

He looked over at the door, saw me standing there and waved. In a minute he hung up, grabbed his baseball cap from the rack, and came over to say hello.

"Come for the bargains?" he said. "I can make you a great deal on a flatbed."

"I saw all the traffic headed your way and decided to follow. I didn't know about this."

"I ran ads last Sunday. Most of the people here are from way out of town," he said. "Not much call around here for farm equipment now that there's no irrigation water."

"Will you sell the land, too?"

"No. I'm converting the fields into RV sites for winter Texans."

"THERE IS NO WATER!" a voice boomed from somewhere outside.

"They're starting a little early," True said, glancing at his watch. "Come on and see how much pent-up anger there is over this water situation." He turned toward the back and I went along, curious.

"The Valley Growers Association called me and asked if they could hold a demonstration," True told me as we walked along the hallway toward the back door. "They're trying to organize a one-day shutdown of every port-of-entry from here to Brownsville to draw attention to the water war, that's what they're calling it. That's about the only way we're going to get either of our governments to do more than just make promises they don't keep. The farmers and campesinos are working together. It's an international effort."

Outside, in the hot sun, a man with a bullhorn again thundered the phrase, "THERE IS NO WATER! The men who'd been looking over the farm equipment were coming around the corner of the building, joining the small crowd already gathered in the fallow field. The speaker, one of eight men standing on the back of the flatbed truck, was perhaps fifty, as lean and dry as the desiccated land around us.

"And why is there no water?" said a wiry brown man, pushing his face close to the microphone. "Because Presidente Vicente Fox is deaf to our needs. We, the farmers of Tamaulipas, have been protesting in front of Mexico's National Water Commission for three weeks. AND NOTHING HAS HAPPENED! THERE IS NO WATER! We come here from Matamoros and Reynosa to join you in demanding the water treaty BE ENFORCED NOW!"

I shaded my eyes with my hand as I listened and looked at these people planning a blockade of international bridges to try and get the attention of two governments. Before Zanjiv Mehendru's murder, much of the anger these men felt had been aimed at him after a reporter had quoted him as saying that under the conditions of extreme drought, Mexico had a right to exercise "flexibility" in complying with its water-treaty obligations and that the United States was better equipped to cope with the economic disaster than was Mexico.

The reality was that only Chichuahua State benefitted from the water hoarding. Downstream both American and Mexican Farmers were desperate for water, one of the reasons for their having brought their protest here.

If one of these desperate, frustrated growers had shot Zanjiv Mehendru, he'd gotten away with it because the only police force that could look for the killer had arrested my husband. I said good-bye to True and turned away. I wanted to go home.

THIRTY-TWO

Monday, June 3

Holding rifles, the judiciales stood in a line in front of the municipal building. They had arrived in three Jetta vans, scattering the demonstrators Olivia had arranged for the hearing. Santo Girón, the chief of police, had responded by sending his own men. They had lined up on the opposite side of the street facing the judiciales. Standing with legs spread, their hands rested on the holstered pistols that hung from the gun belts hugging their hips. Drivers passing by craned their necks at the sight, some braking and backing up rather than negotiating the block between two lines of armed men.

What do they think this is?" Enrique said, as he escorted me into the building. "The gunfight at the OK Corral?"

Mercedes Solar, seated at the back of the hearing room, gave me an encouraging smile as I walked with Enrique down the aisle to the front, where the Berreras and Barton Howard were seated already. The same man in shirtsleeves who'd been piling papers on the magistrate's bench at the first hearing stood in front of the chamber door, his arms folded, casually watchful, playing the dual role of bailiff and bodyguard.

Enrique Vera looked excited, eyeing Alfonso Carmin as if the state prosecutor had lost the case already. At ten-forty, Tito Berg swept into the room and made his way to the defense table to scattered applause from the spectators. A couple of the judiciales standing at attention inside the courtroom dropped their pose to walk over to shake his hand. The atomic ant was a celebrity.

Berg wore a light gray suit, a pale pink shirt with French cuffs fastened by large gold cuff links, and a tie with a design of red hibiscus and bright green leaves that seemed to leap off the black silk. He placed his monogrammed briefcase in the center of the scarred defense table with the sublime air of a seasoned actor placing a prop, then motioned to Enrique to join him before pulling out the wooden chair and sitting down. He ignored Carmin, who sat at the prosecutor's table straightening his yellow tie against the pale blue of his shirt.

The bench seats creaked as the people in the courtroom turned to get a good look at Clay walking in between the two black-uniformed prison guards. Several of the crowd held up signs in his support, but if Clay saw them, he didn't react. I had cut his hair on my last visit and it didn't look too bad, but his blue suit hung loosely on him, as if borrowed from a bigger man. He'd lost so much weight that he'd had to punch a new hole in his belt to cinch it tight enough to hold up his pants.

The man in shirtsleeves jumped at some sound unheard by the rest of us and opened the communicating door for Magistrado Resendez, who marched in without glancing at his audience. He seated himself, folding his hands before him, his eyes darting around the room, settling on Tito Berg, whom he acknowledged with a deep nod of his head before moving on to stare at the prosecutor.

"Licenciado Carmin," he said.

Alfonso Carmin, on his feet, replied, "Magistrado—"

Tito Berg stood as he said, "If I may speak, Magistrado . . ."

"Certainly, licenciado Berg," Resendez said.

"I request that the court make an immediate ruling to release Señor Jones for lack of evidence. No weapon has been found linking my client to the murder. No proof has been offered that my client even knew the dead man. No motive has been offered as to why a successful doctor of veterinary medicine, living over fifty miles from here, should drive all the way to Ojinaga to murder the victim when both lived within thirty miles of each other, one of them, the victim, on an isolated ranch where the body might have gone undetected for many weeks. The prosecutor has no scientific evidence. Señor Jones's fingerprints were not found on or in the victim's pickup. There was no gunshot residue, no lead or barium detected on his—"

"You can't expect his hands to have had gunshot residue. The man was arrested six weeks after the murder," Carmin said.

"Exactly," Berg answered triumphantly. "When the case was so cold that the judiciales had to grab up an innocent man or go home to Chihuahua empty-handed."

"We have an eyewitness to the murder," Carmin said.

"Ah, yes, the eyewitness. The prosecutor's office has refused to give me access to this Aida Machuca so that I may question her, but I don't need to ask her anything when I have documents and reputable witnesses to show that she was incarcerated at the time of the murder."

Resendez pulled at his beard and shifted his eyes from Berg to Carmin almost pleadingly.

"The jail records are wrong," Carmin said. "The witness

was released from custody at eight P.M. on the twenty-third of February."

"So three people are wrong, including the jailer!" Berg waved a sheaf of papers in the air. "The testimony of my witnesses will refute this nonsense that Aida Machuca could have seen anything other than another prisoner scrawling an obscenity on the wall of the holding cell."

"Then I suppose we must hear them," Resendez said, sounding about as enthusiastic as a man agreeing to go to the ballet with his wife.

The narrow-shouldered man who took the stand was dressed in brown pants and shirt. He removed a green baseball cap with a "Piso Caliente" logo and held it in both hands.

Berg smiled at him and asked his name and occupation.

"Tomas Téllez, jailer."

"You were on duty at the city jail the evening of the twenty-second of February, when Aida Machuca was brought in?"

"I was."

"What time was this?" Berg asked.

"I came on duty at three that afternoon. I signed her in at eight P.M."

"Why was she arrested?"

"Public drunkenness."

"Was this the first time she'd been arrested?"

"No, she's a regular."

"How long was she to remain in jail?"

"Forty-eight hours."

"From eight on Friday until eight on Sunday, is that correct?" Berg asked.

"Yes."

"You work three to eleven each night, do you not?"

"Yes."

"And you were there on duty at eight P.M. on Saturday the twenty-third of February?"

"Yes."

"And Aida Machuca was still in the cell?" Berg asked.

"Yes."

"Was she still in the cell at nine?"

"Yes."

"And at ten?"

"Yes."

"And at eleven?"

"Yes."

"In fact," Berg thundered, "Aida Machuca was in that cell all night long. Short of bilocation—and she's no saint—she couldn't have been in the cell *and* in front of the presidencia on the main plaza, now could she?"

There was scattered laughter among the spectators.

The jailer grinned appreciatively at Berg's rhetoric and responded with a firm "No way she was there."

After Téllez, Berg questioned the jailer on the Sunday shift when Machuca was signed out, and the jail administrator, who testified that the records he'd signed as to Machuca's time served were correct and that the jailers could not be mistaken in identifying her because she was regularly jailed for various petty crimes.

As the last witness left the stand, Berg said in a commanding voice, "There are those who owe for murder who haven't set foot in jail. My client owes for no murder, but languishes in jail. This injustice stops now. I have evidence that not only is Aida Machuca a habitual drunk, but a heroin addict and therefore susceptible to being coerced—"

"I don't see that that's relevant," Carmin said, sounding bored.

"Nor do I," Resendez said quickly.

"If it's not relevant, Magistrado, then why is the state hiding her in a drug rehab center in Chihuahua?"

In one smooth motion, Carmin was on his feet. "She is not being hidden, she is being treated."

"So you admit she's an addict! And since when is the state

so compassionate that it pays the very pricey fee for treatment in a private clinic for a street whore? Does this costly treatment include keeping her supplied with heroin? Why have I not been allowed to interview her on behalf of my client?" Berg shouted.

"Magistrado," Carmin said, his voice rising slightly, "the state has new evidence."

Resendez visibly relaxed. Clay slumped in his chair.

"We have the videotape recording of the border crossing taken from the toll booth on the night of the murder. It will prove the suspect was in Ojinaga," Carmin said emphatically, "at the time the killing took place."

Berg turned an astonished face on Carmin and said, "Show it, then, if you have it. Produce it! Let us all look at it!"

"Can you?" Resendez asked timidly.

"I don't have it with me at this time, Magistrado."

Resendez said, "The prosecution must have time to assemble further evidence. The prisoner will be returned to El Cereso." He was off the bench and out the door in a breath. The shirt-sleeved man, his face stiff with solemnity, crossed his arms over his chest and positioned himself in front of the door that had closed on the magistrate's back.

Some of the observers in the courtroom jumped to their feet, shouting angry, sarcastic comments. Clay was taken out, his eyes downcast.

As the courtroom cleared, I went to talk with Berg. "What happens next?"

"I'm going to see Benito Vascón, in person. No more telephone chats with my little friend."

From across the aisle, Alfonso Carmin gave his fellow lawyer a knowing stare. "Go softly. You don't know where this is coming from."

THIRTY-THREE

I was so sure Berg would prevail," Enrique said, looking like a man whose ex-wife has just claimed the lottery prize.

We stood on the street watching the judiciales climb into their vans and depart. The noonday sun bleached the sky and the south wind blew hot and dry. A truck with ranchera music blaring from its speakers sped by and we turned our faces away from the resulting dust cloud. The paleta vendor on the corner was not so lucky. He tossed the grit-coated frozen treat into the street, where a dog snatched it up, and fished in his cart for another to hand his customer.

I said good-bye to Enrique and fled Ojinaga, feeling much as the refugees from the massacre by Pancho Villa's forces must have, relief at escaping, but leaving behind the person I held most dear and frightened by what I might yet face. Tito Berg had been so angered by the magistrate's behavior and the prosecutor's remark that I had no doubt he'd stick by us. His ego was now fully engaged. Whether that would be enough for him, and us, to triumph, I didn't know. He'd told me our best bet was the appeal he'd already filed on the magistrate's ruling that Clay was a viable suspect in the murder. He'd also said it might take six to eight months for the Fifth District Appeals Court in Chihuahua City to rule.

At the trading post, the CLOSED sign was up, meaning that Mike Dodd was out on a call. He might enjoy the work on the ranches and love the locale, but we couldn't expect him to stay on much longer. The money certainly wasn't all that good, as we had reason to know. Nor could we afford to keep buying vet supplies with no income from Mike's calls and next to none from Clay's impromptu clinic at the prison. Those fees barely covered costs after the warden took his share.

I was unlocking the front doors when Jack Raff's pickup pulled in. Lucy Ramos and Claudia Reyes were with him. I tried to smile, but they read my face and knew the hearing had gone badly.

"That Resendez didn't rule against you!" Lucy said.

Claudia rushed up the steps and put her arms around me. "This is terrible. I'm going to double up on my prayers and pester God until he does something. Why don't you come home with me for a while. Some food and company will do you good."

"Thank you, but I need to telephone my father and let him know what's happened."

"What can we do, Texana?" Jack Raff said. The positive note of action in his voice lifted my spirits.

"Nothing," I said mildly, telling them how the magistrate had ignored the two jailers' and the jail administrator's testimony and returned Clay to prison. "Resendez is going to rule against Clay, no matter what. Unless I can find out why he's doing this, and who's bribing or frightening him, Clay's not going to get out."

"Then that's what we'll do," Jack said. "You get some rest. I'll come over tomorrow and we'll talk." He rounded up

Claudia and Lucy, who clearly wanted to stay. I went in and poured myself a large whiskey.

I was sitting at the table watching the elongated shadows creep up the hill behind the trading post when Mike Dodd came in. I offered to fix him a sandwich, but he said he'd eaten with the rancher, who'd called him out to look at one of his horses.

I asked him to sit down. I'd made a hard decision and I wanted to talk it over with him.

"You've done a great job here. You're liked and appreciated," I told him. It was true. He listened to the tales the old borderhands had to tell, he didn't patronize the ranch hands, some of whom knew as much or more than he about doctoring cattle, some of whom only thought they did, and he was comfortable and patient with the in-comers who'd jumped boot-first into ranching with the idea that driving a pickup and wearing a vest made them knowledgeable cattlemen. Perhaps most important, he'd quickly picked up enough border Spanish to get along.

"You going to fire me?" he said.

"Never, but . . . the hearing went against us today and it may be months before Clay's appeal is heard. You've been here almost eight weeks. You have a life you need to be getting on with. I can hardly ask you to give up any more of it."

"The way I see it, I haven't given up anything. I've gained. If I hadn't come here, I'd have stayed in Odessa and spent my days neutering cats and dogs and my nights at the bowling alley. Being here, getting to know this way of life, it's opened a whole new world. I like it out here. I'd like to see things through. Meet Clay when he comes home."

"I'd like nothing better, Mike, but I have to admit, there's a cost factor for us, too."

He raised a hand. "I know where you're going. When you offered me the full vet fee, you were too generous. I've kept a record of the wholesale costs of the medicines and supplies I've used. That money is coming back to you."

"Mike, I can't—"

"No arguments. It's what's fair. I get paid for my time, you get the money you're out for supplies. After all, you're providing room and board, too."

"Probably I should argue with you, but I won't. I want Clay to come home with his practice intact. And he'd hate to let down the ranchers who depend on us."

Mike smiled, looking as happy as a kid with a free day from school. Phobe picked that moment to leap onto his lap, as if she were small enough to fit. She kneaded her big paws against his chest. He rubbed her long back, while on the floor Jefe jumped up and down like a spring-loaded toy.

For a moment, I was almost happy.

THIRTY-FOUR

Tuesday, June 4

I set a bacon omelet in front of Mike Dodd and poured out the coffee, adding half-and-half generously to mine.

"You aren't eating?" he said.

"I had toast with my first cup of coffee at five-thirty."

I sat back and looked around the bright room, so different from the old trading post with its thick beams and wood walls. Clay and I had outlined the foundation of this building with rocks, the only "blueprint" we had used. I'd put in as many windows as possible. Only on the north, the direction of winter's wind, and the west, to protect against the setting sun, did we omit the light. The old adobero, who'd come from Ojinaga, had made the walls three feet thick. I'd insisted on a peaked roofline and a metal roof to reflect the heat. Except in the searing temperatures of July and August, ceiling fans kept us comfortably cool.

I was washing up when the bell jingled. I dried my hands and went out to wait on my first customer of the day.

Jack Raff came marching in wearing his habitual T-shirt, shorts, and sandals. This T-shirt was lime green with a stylized Virgin of Guadalupe on the front.

"I'm ready to get started brainstorming over what we know about Mehendru," he announced.

I made another pot of coffee and a plate of buttered toast. Mike took himself and Phobe and Jefe off to the clinic. After Jack had eaten all the toast and my kidneys were floating with coffee, we settled in to go over all the information I'd accumulated about Zanjiv Mehendru, which meant I did a lot of talking, including mentioning how Mehendru had treated old Flaco Ordaz over the garbage dump as well as the fact that he had turned Jip Jackson in to the feds.

"Unyielding, wasn't he?" Jack said.

"There may have been a reason for that," I said, telling Jack about Mehendru's stepfather, Aurelio Blancas, and the murder of Mercedes Solar's father and brother.

"Poor young man," Jack said. "Worse than a death to find those you love corrupt and vile. And the mother, too selfish to act when confronted with a truth she must have been ignoring for many years. Amazing what we'll put up with to stay comfortable."

"She may have been too afraid to act," I said, thinking of the kind of revenge a man like Blancas would exact for betrayal.

I showed Jack the clippings on Mehendru from the *International,* the *El Diario de Chihuahua* article, and the notes I'd taken on Grupo Prima.

"I keep coming back to the Blancases," I said, "if only because they're the most powerful people with a connection to Mehendru. The prosecutor warned Tito Berg to be careful. He as good as said someone very powerful was behind what's going on in that court. But the Blancases had nothing to gain from Mehendru's death and nothing to fear from him. No way Aurelio could be made to pay for killing Mercedes Solar's father and brother now. No authority in Mexico would dare touch him. And what else was there that Mehendru might have known?"

"What about Mercedes Solar?" Jack asked. "Could she have harbored such hatred of the family that killed her father and brother that she somehow blamed Mehendru, too?"

"Her grief at his death seemed genuine to me. He thought enough of her to put her in his will."

"Guilt."

"That's what she said."

"Love betrayed is more dangerous than indifference."

"I wonder if Zanjiv Mehendru ever loved his stepfather. He was only seven when his father died. The mother remarried soon after. Blancas should have been important in his life."

"A man like Blancas couldn't love another man's child. More likely, he resented him," Jack said. "The fact that his stepfather was a murderer might not have been such a great shock to young Zanjiv Mehendru. He was intelligent. He had a mind for scholarship. He must have observed things at home, heard things, known things. What the Solar killings might have done was give him a justifiable reason for breaking all ties with his stepfather, even if it meant losing his mother, too."

It was close to noon when we finished talking, having drawn no conclusion, found no one fact that seemed to point in any particular direction, either at who might have killed Mehendru, or who might be framing Clay.

I shoved the scattered clippings and my notes back into the folder and invited Jack to stay for lunch. He begged off, having promised to visit friends during the afternoon. After he left, I went into the back to prepare something for Mike. While I fished out sliced brisket from the freezer to microwave, it dawned on me that I hadn't had a single customer during the morning. I was wrapping tortillas around portions of shredded brisket when I heard the bell. I put the burrito with the others on a platter and went back to the front. Dennis Bustamante was striding toward me down the center aisle, looking pleased and excited about something.

"Have you heard about what happened this morning?" he said, stopping in front of the counter. "Everybody from Polvo came driving down O'Reilly Street, lights flashing and horns honking, kids standing in the beds of the pickups wearing T-shirts with Clay's picture and waving flags. They headed for the bridge. Somebody used a bullhorn to announce they were marching into Ojinaga to protest Clay's imprisonment."

"You're kidding."

Dennis shook his head. "You must have heard them driving by early this morning."

"I was in back," I said, "and the adobe's so thick it muffles road noise."

"I wish you could have seen it," Dennis said. "I followed them in the department car to make sure there was no trouble. People were coming out of the stores along O'Reilly to see what was going on and joining them on foot. By the time they reached the bridge, there must have been close to three, maybe four hundred. Somebody on duty at the bridge evidently radioed the judiciales as soon as he saw the crowd coming, 'cause just as they got to the end of the bridge, four vans pulled up. The judiciales poured out like clowns in a circus act, except these guys had guns. They warned the crowd to turn around and go back. Said if they came onto Mexican soil there'd be trouble. The crowd stopped. You won't believe what they did next. Willie Zuniga's band was set up in the bed of his pickup. He'd written a corrido about Clay's arrest. They sang it right there."

"What's a corrido?" Mike's curious voice said from behind me. He'd come in while Dennis was talking.

"A ballad," Dennis told him. "The best ones celebrate border legends, people like Gregorio Cortez and Pancho Villa. And now, Clay Jones."

Not the most favorable of precedents. Gregorio Cortez had died in jail after being poisoned. Villa had been gunned down by seven riflemen on orders from the revolutionary government he'd helped bring to power. I concentrated hard on keeping an amiable expression on my face, but things were getting too emotional, too public, too close to being out of control.

"There wasn't any trouble?" I said. "No one got hurt? Or arrested?"

"Nah," Dennis said. "After the music, the folks on foot started back and the drivers backed their vehicles up. The only ones disappointed were the judiciales."

The door opened. Friends and neighbors poured in, all talking at once, telling me about the protest march, excited and pleased with themselves for doing something. Though I had serious doubts of the wisdom of such an action, I understood how they felt and loved them for it. Two and three at a time, more people arrived. We turned it into a party. Mike helped me with chips and canned dip, I brought out the brisket burritos and made more. They sang the "Ballad of Clay Jones" for me. If we couldn't celebrate Clay's freedom, we celebrated the affection we had for one another.

The last pickup had left and I was trying to sweep crumbs from the floor while Phobe played Swat the Broom, when the telephone rang.

"Conner West has signed a contract for your land," Eileen Washington said, "and given me a check for five thousand dollars earnest money. Can you come in sometime soon and sign the contract?"

West was one of three people Eileen had brought out for me to drive over the place and the one I'd have bet was the least likely to buy. When we'd reached the high point of my land, with its sweeping view of the river, West had made his only remark of the day beyond 'Hello,' when he announced, "I've seen enough." What I'd taken as dismissal apparently had been a decision.

I made mine. "I'll be there at nine-thirty Thursday."

THIRTY-FIVE

Wednesday, June 5

Warden Martinez greeted me at the gate of El Cereso. A healthier, filled-out Zapata curled around our feet, adroitly avoiding being stepped on by any of the visitors.

"I don't know what is going on with that damned magistrado," he said disgustedly. "You take your visit in my office today. I'll get Señor Clay."

As we passed through the compound, several of the other prisoners nodded to me, sympathy clear in their eyes. Word over the fate of any prisoner spread quickly among the other men at El Cereso. The guards at Monday's hearing would have told the others what they had witnessed in the courtroom.

A guard deferentially held open the door into the hall. In his office, the warden offered me his desk chair and left. I put the sack of sandwiches I'd brought for Clay on the table and sat down, nervously drumming my heels on the floor as I waited. I kept my eyes on the door until he walked in and we were alone for the first time in fifty-four days. I knew, I'd marked them off on the calendar. I went straight to him and we held each other for a long moment.

Talking into my hair, Clay tried to sound optimistic, saying perhaps the next hearing would be different.

Let's sit down," I said. "I don't know about you, but I feel like I'm reeling still from what happened." I pulled the desk chair around close to Clay's, where I could touch his hand.

He spoke first and surprised me with the subject. "You say Mike Dodd likes it out here? He's enjoying the work and the people?"

"He loves it. Why?" I asked.

"Does he like it enough to buy the practice?" Clay said. "That way, you'd have something to live on if I have to stay in here."

"Don't talk like that."

"We have to be realistic."

"You're being precipitous."

"Talk it over with him. See if he's interested."

I didn't argue, but I didn't plan on acting on the suggestion.

"You go home now," Clay said, standing up. "You need some rest. I'm okay."

"Your lunch," I said.

He took the sack. "Don't worry about me. I'm all right, but just now, I need to be alone."

I left, trying to be understanding of his dismissal of me. Clay had lost hope. For the first time in our marriage, I felt absolutely alone, cut off from the person who was the other half of me.

THIRTY-SIX

Thursday, June 6

I left the trading post after breakfast, but rather than going to Presidio and then up Highway 67 to Marfa, I took Pinto Canyon Road through the Chinati Mountains. This route saves a few miles, but no time, since the road is unpaved for half its forty-eight miles. The route is scenic. Except for the hum of a Border Patrol helicopter passing overhead, I was alone until I reached the edge of Marfa.

Eileen Washington was at her desk, making notes on a yellow pad. She had rearranged enough paperwork to make room for a large Styrofoam cup of frothy coffee that smelled of sugar and vanilla. I slid into the only other chair and inhaled the fragrant aroma.

"Want some?" she said. "Get a cup from the closet."

I couldn't resist. It was four steps to the closet that was storage for office supplies and a copy machine. I lifted the top cup from a tilted stack and carried it back to the desk. Eileen poured half the fragrant coffee from her cup into mine. It was wonderful, rich with whipped cream and vanilla bean.

"Your buyer came to see me on the recommendation of one of my Houston clients," Eileen said, "before I even advertised your place." She reached around to the small table squeezed in between her chair and the window and thumbed through a stack of papers, extracting one bunch clipped together and handing it to me.

"This is a standard real estate contract. Since there are no easements involved and no buildings, and the buyer's paying cash, it's fairly straightforward. I told Mr. West that it was customary out here to accept the property as originally surveyed, so all that has to be resurveyed is the forty acres you're retaining."

Eileen went over the contract with me page by page to make sure I understood. She'd also prepared a summary of my estimated costs, which she handed me. After closing costs, her six-percent fee, and capital-gains taxes, I would have roughly $258,000.

"Are you pleased?" she asked.

"Oh, yes," I said. "I've never had enough money before to exceed the Federal Deposit Insurance limit."

"Well, now you can use three banks," she said, smiling and handing me a pen. "Too bad Marfa only has one."

I signed my name on the last page, initialed each of the others.

"The closing can be as soon as you like after the title search is done, which shouldn't take more than a couple of weeks," she said. "I talked to the surveyor and he's agreed to put you at the top of his list and have the survey done by that time."

Eileen put my copy of the contract into a manila folder, handed it to me, and we were done. As the door to her office was swinging closed behind me, I saw Mack Friedel, the water-board chairman, standing in front of his office across the street having a cigarette. I waved, got into the pickup, put the key in the ignition, then sat there, motor running.

I don't believe in intuition. I think what we call intuition is knowledge, based on experience, reacting with new data so that the mind makes a leap to a conclusion. Seeing Friedel triggered one of those leaps. I cut the motor, got out, and crossed the street.

Friedel removed the cigarette from his mouth, cupping it in his hand, and gave me a polite inquiring look as I walked up.

"Good morning. May we talk inside for a few minutes?" I asked him.

"Sure thing," he said, throwing the half-smoked cigarette down and rubbing it out with the toe of his shoe.

"I didn't mean to make you waste your cigarette."

"I'm trying to quit. Come on in," he said, holding the office door open for me.

I walked over to the same wall map of the county we'd looked at on my first visit. He closed the door and drew the blinds against the morning sun that was angling straight in with a blinding glare.

"When I was here the first time, you traced these," I said, connecting the marked wells in my general area as he'd done that day. "And you said the water board is going to publish a report."

"Yes," Friedel said, "charts and maps. All the hydrologist's findings, and fifty-year supply-and-demand projections."

"So the report is finished but not available to the public yet, is that right?"

"Right. It'll be some weeks yet before we announce a public meeting to present the results and release the information."

"Could you tell me how long it's been since the hydrologist completed his report?"

Friedel scowled. "These things take time. The newspaper has made entirely too much of how slow we've—"

"You misunderstand me," I said placatingly. "I'm not complaining. I know committee work goes slowly. I personally think it's better to take the time to get it right, don't you?"

The scowl left his face. "Nice to have someone understand."

"I know the report is confidential."

"It wouldn't do to have it leak out," he said. "This sort of information can impact property values tremendously."

"All I really would like to know is exactly when the hydrologist's report was handed over to you and when the other board members got a look at it."

"I don't see what harm it would do to tell you that," he said slowly. Going around to the desk, he pulled out a leather-bound notebook, turned through the pages until he found what he was looking for. "The hydrologist finished up his fieldwork last fall, at the end of November, to be exact." Friedel turned over more pages. "He faxed us his written report on January sixteenth. Some of the board had questions and there was some follow-up—"

"All the board members had copies of the report?" I said. "Yes."

"Including Zanjiv Mehendru?"

"Yes, of course."

"Thank you, Mr. Friedel, you've been very helpful."

I spent the two hours and twenty minutes it took to drive home thinking about what to do next. I hoped that I'd come up with at least a part of the truth and prayed that somehow it would help Clay if I could find an answer to the question I'd formulated after talking with Friedel.

I'd been home only a few minutes when Mike, in a blood-splattered shirt and smiling broadly, came into the trading post.

"What's all that?" I asked, indicating the blood.

"A rancher's dog went after a porcupine. I had to anesthetize him to get all the spines out. I'm keeping an eye on him until he comes out of the anesthetic."

"Clay gets one of those cases every couple of years, usually when someone buys a dog that hasn't been raised out here," I said. "Poor pups have to learn the hard way."

"You had a telephone call. Hold on while I get it." He went back into the clinic and came out with a slip of paper. "He called once before."

"Thanks, Mike. You're doing triple duty—vet, sales clerk, answering service. I hope we can make it up to you." I glanced down at the note: Edmund Cutler. I slipped the note into my pant pocket.

"Soaking that shirt in sweet milk will get the bloodstains out," I told Mike.

Phobe and Jefe came running to meet me. Phobe bumped my leg with her head and gave a deep throaty purr. Jefe licked my hand as I bent to pick her up. When she's excited by a homecoming she tends to get underfoot and I'm always afraid that I'll step on her, so she's carried much of the time.

I deposited her in one of the chairs and Phobe jumped on the arm and sharpened her claws on the upholstery. I looked up Jack Raff's number and telephoned.

"Come for lunch," I told him. "I have an idea I want to run by you."

THIRTY-SEVEN

Jack Raff tilted his head back and drained his glass of iced tea. We'd finished the cheeseburgers and fried onion rings. The best I could offer for desert was a Hostess cupcake. Mike ate his with alacrity, saying he needed to get back to his patient, the dog recovering from his run-in with the porcupine.

"Nice young man," Jack said. "He fits in out here."

I waited until he'd finished his cupcake, then said, "Come into the front. I want to show you something."

As I passed the counter out front, I grabbed a pencil. My copy of the Presidio County map hangs on the north wall of the trading post. I stood in front of it and drew a line connecting those marked water wells and springs that Mack Friedel had noted on my first visit to his office. I stepped back. The oblong shape I'd marked encompassed three of the area's largest ranches, Bill Picket's Bar J, Lost Creek, and the Motts' Ranch, and dozens of small landowners along the river, including all of Polvo and my place. Right in the middle was Choke Canyon.

"An odd blob of a shape," Jack said. "What's it mean?"

"I'm not sure. The growers demonstrating at True Jackson's liquidation auction kept repeating one catchphrase, 'There is no water.' They meant the Rio Grande, of course, but the phrase stuck in my mind. It got me to thinking, because it's what we've always believed out here—drill a well and the odds are against hitting water. Move over ten feet from a good well and drill another and there's no water. But what if there were? What if there's an untapped aquifer deep under this land?" I said.

"Land values'd shoot up," Jack said. "Is there water?"

"I don't know, but I think the Tri-County Water Planning Board does. Everyone laughed last summer when they announced plans to bring in a hydrologist to map possible aquifers in the region. I think their report, when it's made public, will say their expert found at least one aquifer. Somewhere here." I pointed to the blob, as Jack had called it.

"How does this tie in with Mehendru?" Jack asked. "I assume that's where you're going with this?"

I went to my desk and got out the Tri-County Water Planning Board business card I picked up on my first visit to the office and handed it to Jack.

"Zanjiv Mehendru was a board member. According to Friedel, Mehendru had a copy of the hydrologist's report at least a month before he died. Eileen Washington told me the Motts and Bill Picket have sold their ranches. She didn't know to whom. Hugger Baines told me that a woman from an environmental group had approached him about donating his land to them. He couldn't recall the name, but I think it may have been Christiana Jacobs of Bonis Avidus. Mike told me that these environmental groups often do flyovers of land they're interested in. If Bonis Aidus did a flyover of this area, they would have known about the spring. That alone would make them interested in acquiring Hugger's place. A second person showed up trying to persuade Hugger to sell his land. He described the young man as 'a guy in a ponytail.' "

"Crosse Hickman."

"I think there's a possibility that Bonis Avidus not only did the flyover, but also found out about the hydrologist's report. If so, they're buying up land before the owners know they may be sitting on top of a lake of water."

Jack's face was grave. "So now you find out—"

"Who bought the Motts' and Bill Picket's ranches. And I'm going to ask Kate Worthy, the other big landowner, if anyone has tried to buy her out. If only one answer is Bonis Avidus, it may be a coincidence. If two or three, then it's at least suspicious."

"Why only the big ranches?" Jack asked. "Wouldn't these people want the small places, too?"

"No. Once they own the majority of the land, they could drill all the wells they wanted and pump the water right out from under the smallholdings like mine. Think about how El Paso bought that big ranch in Hudspeth County just to get the water rights. 'Water ranching,' they call it. The wells they pump are lowering the water table on the surrounding ranches."

"If it turns out that Christiana Jacobs or Crosse have approached these people," Jack said, "then what?"

"I'll try to find out if Zanjiv Mehendru thought the environmental group had inside information."

"If he did, he'd have gone public," Jack said. "He'd have denounced them like a preacher casting out harlots."

THIRTY-EIGHT

Friday, June 7

I drove the sweep of land toward the empty horizon to a cattle guard with a sign inked on a plain square of tin wired to the fence: MOTT RANCH, HEADQUARTERS 2 MILES, an unprepossessing entrance to a sixty-five-section ranch.

Three chocolate Labradors ran to meet me as I approached the house. A man came out onto the porch and called them back as I parked and got out. J.L. Mott is tall and rangy, with white hair and blue eyes as faded as stonewashed jeans. His family has ranched this land for four generations. I know him to be unassuming and kind, a man who works as hard as the day hands he hires to help him cull, brand, and doctor his cattle.

I hadn't called first. The questions I had to ask, personal and none of my business, were best done in person. No is an easy word on the telephone. I joined J.L. and the dogs on the wide porch. The animals sniffed around my boots and ankles, intrigued by scents of bobcat and another unknown dog. Satisfied, one licked my hand. All three settled around our feet in well-behaved fashion as J.L. invited me to sit down and offered me coffee.

It was just after ten o'clock. I'd left home at eight-thirty, my only breakfast the half-and-half I'd added to my standard two cups of strong coffee.

J.L. called Betty, his wife, to bring the pot and another cup for the company, then took a chair, told me how sorry he was about Clay's situation, and soundly condemned what he called "those idiots over there."

By that time, Betty, a white-haired women with a sweet face and a generous nature, had brought the coffee. She asked about Clay.

I gave them a capsuled version of the hearings.

"We read in the *International* about that so-called witness and her lies. It's a shame," Betty said. "I think Mr. Mehendru would be the first to condemn that prosecutor and judge. He seemed like such a forthright man. I was shocked when I read about the murder. He visited us just the week before he died."

"Mr. Mehendru came to see you?" I said.

"On a Sunday afternoon," J.L. said. "You know, one day is pretty much like another out here, but Sunday is the only day I don't ride the pastures to check on the herd."

Betty said, "Mr. Mehendru wanted to know if anyone had been around asking to buy our ranch."

"I thought for a minute he wanted to buy it," J.L. said. "Asked him if he'd come to outbid the other fellow."

"The other fellow?" I said.

"Those were Mehendru's very words!" J.L. said. "Crosse Hickman, I told him. I didn't think much of Crosse at first, because of the ponytail, but he's a sensible fellow in spite of it. Gave us a fair price and the contract allows us to stay on as caretakers for a year, so we can take our time about moving into town. Change at our age is a little rough."

My stomach did a heave and I felt acid in my throat. I swallowed and asked Betty if she had any Pepcid. "I guess I had too much coffee on an empty stomach."

"I have some Tums," she said, looking concerned. "Will that do?"

"I'll take four," I told her.

She got up, returning in a few minutes with the tablets and a plate of peanut butter and crackers.

"I thought you ought to eat something," she said, setting the plate on the metal table by my chair.

I chewed the antacids and ate two of the crackers. When my stomach stopped making waves, I said, "I heard that you'd sold, but I thought maybe it was just a rumor."

"Signed the contract two months ago," J.L. said.

"I sold some of my land yesterday," I told them.

"It's a hard decision, isn't it," Betty said, reaching to take her husband's hand. "We debated for months. But between the drought and cattle prices, we're losing money just paying the taxes. If we hadn't sold, the children would have had to in order to pay the estate taxes after we're gone."

I visited with the Motts for a half hour more, asking after their grandchildren. Betty showed me pictures of the oldest grandson's graduation from Marfa High School only a few weeks earlier.

After the Motts, I stopped at Lost Creek Ranch, the next place on my list. The owner, Kate Worthy, had inherited the ranch from her parents and operated it on her own ever since. We talked in the barn, where she was rubbing down the horse she'd ridden fence on that morning. She, too, had been visited by Crosse Hickman.

"The first time was in January or early February," she said, as she ran the brush in long firm strokes down the horse's side. "Crosse chatted about the history of the ranch, knew enough to ask questions, and not silly ones. He's smooth, I'll give him that. He listens well and takes in what you say so he can ask more questions. Before you know it, you're telling him things about your own place that you probably shouldn't. He made two visits before he got around to discussing buying the place. Said he was authorized to offer a little over market value." She paused in the brushing. "When I told him I didn't want to sell, he became very insistent. Pushy, really. He came back twice after that. The last time maybe a month ago. He said he could work a deal where I could stay on for my lifetime. I told him I hadn't ever lived on land I didn't own and I wasn't going to. I hope he doesn't come back. I'm not sure he knows how to take no for an answer."

"Zanjiv Mehendru," I said, "did he drop by around the same time as Crosse's first visit?"

"How did you know that?" Kate said, giving the bay gelding a pat on the rump as she put away the brush. "He showed up early one morning, asking about anyone who'd been trying to buy my place. He seemed real upset when I mentioned Crosse. I told him I thought that Hickman had talked to almost everybody around here. The Motts and Bill Picket sold out to him, you know."

Which saved me a trip to the Bar J. Zanjiv Mehendru had been on the same quest I was on.

I spent the drive home working out what to do next. Once home, I telephoned the office of Bonis Avidus in Fort Davis. Christiana Jacobs answered. I lied, telling her that I had some land her environmental group might be interested in. She suggested I come to her office on Monday morning so we could discuss it.

THIRTY-NINE

Sunday, June 9

Saturday afternoon at five the temperature had hit 102 degrees. I'd filled water bottles and placed them in the freezer to have ready for Clay this morning.

After breakfast, I folded Clay's clean laundry into a bag and then did a few household chores. At nine-thirty, I loaded the cooler with the frozen water bottles and packed apples, peanut butter, and crackers for Clay's lunch. It seemed to take all my energy to carry the cooler to the pickup. With each successive trip, the drive seemed more punishing, the time on the road longer, my stamina less.

In Presidio, someone, perhaps inspired by the demonstration at the bridge, had suspended a FREE CLAY JONES banner over O'Reilly Street in the spot where, every May, the Onion Festival banner hung. There'd been no festival this year because there'd been no crop.

In Ojinaga, the first thing I saw was Enrique Vera's Xterra parked in front of El Cereso. He waited for me with the motor running and the air conditioner going. Across the street in the doorway of La Bola de Oro, the same fat, shirtless man who was there every Sunday sat in his chair reading a folded newspaper, a bottle of beer in one hand.

I envied the fat man his complacency. I undid my seat belt, slid out of the pickup, locked the door, and anxiously crossed the street. Enrique saw me coming and got out. He wore a wine red cotton shirt, stonewashed jeans, and polished boots. I couldn't read anything from his neutral expression.

"You've heard something from Berg?" I said.

"Yes," he said. "Let's sit in the car out of this heat."

We got in the Xterra. Enrique turned slightly to face me. "Friday, Tito found out that José Cabello, the assistant attorney general, specifically selected the Fifth District magistrado who'll hear Clay's appeal.

"Meaning the decision is foregone against Clay," I said.

"Exactly. Tito is going to refile the appeal in the Sixth District and ask that Magistrado Antonia de Juana make the ruling. They were classmates in college."

"Will this appeal go any faster?"

"I have the impression that Tito's been keeping the magistrado personally apprised about the case. I think we have a good chance. Also, Olivia told me to be sure and tell you that the mayor has one of the JUSTICE FOR JONES posters in his office window. He came to her and asked if she wanted him to have the water department find a 'break' in the waterline in front of Magistrado Resendez's house that it would take a few weeks to fix."

I laughed. "What did she tell him?"

"She said it was a good idea and to hold it in reserve."

"Talk about bringing pressure to bear," I said.

"Olivia thought you would appreciate it."

Ever the gentleman, Enrique walked me back to my pickup to fetch the cooler and insisted on carrying it inside the gate for me. The gatekeeper no longer checked anything I brought in and the guards all knew me by name. I was worried when Clay wasn't there to meet me, but I saw why when I got to his cell. He was seated on the cot cradling a fuzzy baby emu in his lap. The fan was fixed on them, but the hot air it blew was anything but cooling. Clay dripped sweat and the mute emu had its beak open in an attempt to cool itself. I broke out the frozen water bottles. Clay told me to take two, put them in one of his shirts, and place them so they rested on either side of the emu. He put one at his back.

"That feels great. Thanks," he said. "The emu isn't sick. Whoever dropped it at the gate just didn't want it."

The baby bird was the size of a small dog, its down a pale gray. As Clay stroked its neck and back, it looked up at him, blinking its big eyes.

"What are you going to do with it?" I asked.

"The warden knows a man who keeps a few emu. He lives right by the river about a little ways west of the bridge. I thought maybe you could drop it off on your way. The man's name is Tipo. He's got a shed there with a corral behind, I'm told. You can put the emu on his side in the cooler. It won't hurt for the little time it will take you to get there."

"Okay, I'll make the emu-run," I said, earning a smile.

The smile got bigger when I told Clay what Enrique had said about the new appeal.

"I feel better knowing Berg has enough influence to get a particular magistrate to hear the appeal," Clay said. "That's the best news—no, the only good news we've had."

After lunch, we put the emu in the cooler, leaving the drain hole open so it could get air. Thankful these birds are mute, I left El Cereso and headed for the bridge. A quarter mile before I reached it, a dirt road turned off. I followed it along the riverbed west for half a mile to a sheet-metal-and-wood-frame shack. A skinny little man sat in a propped-back chair under the shade of the overhang, his arms folded over his chest, eyes closed, mouth hanging open in sleep. To one side of the shack, in a small enclosure, three adult emu paced back and forth, their plumy feathers molting in big patches. I drove right past and headed for a crossing point I knew of. "No way I leave you there," I said to the cooler-encased emu. I doubted the adults would survive the summer.

I crossed the Rio Grande illegally, doubly so because I was bringing in fauna, as customs would call the baby emu. The drive home was uneventful. The only other vehicle on the road was a Border Patrol four-by-four dragging a tire to smooth the sand so that in the morning it could be checked for fresh tracks of illegals crossing on foot. I turned into the trading post parking lot and drove around to the back. A blue Volvo was parked next to Clay's green pickup and Mike's white Honda Civic.

Crosse Hickman and Mike sat in the soft shade of the big mesquite tree. As I cut the motor, Crosse stood up and walked in my direction.

I turned my back to him to push the captain's seat forward, unlatch the cooler lid, and lifted out the baby emu. When I turned around, Crosse was right behind me.

"Look at that," Crosse said, reaching out. The baby emu thrust both strong legs at him in the only protective gesture the flightless birds have, its thick claws leaving red welts on the back of his hand.

"Son of a bitch!" Crosse yelled, pleasantness evaporating in pain and anger.

Mike came to the rescue of the bird, taking it from me.

"Come in and I'll put some antiseptic on that," I told Crosse. He was looking after Mike, who was taking the bird into the clinic. "I'd like to wring its neck," he said.

I asked him to wait on the narrow back porch a minute. Phobe and Jefe hovered just inside the door, needy for attention. I got out their food, took them into the laundry room where their baskets were, and bribed them with an early meal to stay there quietly. I closed the door behind me. Crosse was in no mood to have a bobcat jump in his lap.

I opened the screen door and told him to come in. "Wash your hand with that soap over by the sink while I get the antiseptic," I said, going to the bathroom for the tube of ointment Clay kept there.

I inspected his hand. No broken skin. I spread a small amount of the opaque ointment on the three welts. "That'll take care of it," I said. "Sit down and I'll get us both a glass of iced tea."

"Thanks," he said, sitting in the closest armchair. "Sorry to show up unannounced like this on a Sunday, but I wanted to talk to you without a customer walking in."

"What about?" I said, opening the freezer compartment and taking out a tray of ice.

"About Choke Canyon Ranch."

I twisted the blue plastic tray and the ice tubes tumbled loudly into the bowl. I put down the empty tray and turned around to look at Crosse.

"What about it?" I said.

"My people want to buy it," he said. "It would be a tremendous acquisition environmentally. And I thought the cash might be particularly useful to you right now."

"Crosse, I don't own Choke Canyon. You know that."

He smiled. "Technically, no. It belongs to your husband, but I can hardly talk to him, can I."

I leaned back against the counter and stared at him. "I have no idea what you're talking about."

He blinked and stirred in his chair. "You really don't, do you? Sorry, but Edmund Cutler said he'd notified you of the inheritance by letter."

It took me a minute to remember the name. Cutler was the person who'd telephoned a couple of times when I was out and left his name and number with Mike, asking me to get in touch. When I hadn't, he must have written. The letter would be in our box at the tiny post office in the front room of Lucy Ramos's house in Polvo. I couldn't remember the last time I'd emptied it. The amount of mail we get is negligible and I'd been too consumed by Clay's situation to worry about junk mail.

I went over and sat in the armchair nearest Crosse. "You're telling me that Hugger Baines left Choke Canyon to Clay?"

"Yes. We've been hoping to acquire the land as part of the nature preserve for some time. I tried to persuade Mr. Baines to sell, but he wasn't interested."

"No, I can see why not," I said. "A nature preserve wouldn't want mules."

"We were willing to be accommodating," Crosse said. "Now, maybe we can accommodate you. Mr. Baines told me he had no family, so after he died, I called around and located his lawyer. Cutler didn't see the harm in giving me Clay's name, since it might be to his advantage."

I had no trouble believing what Crosse said about locating Hugger's lawyer by the simple process of calling and asking. There were only three people practicing law in Marfa, and one of them specialized in criminal defense. Other than that, there were three or four Houston attorneys who lived there part-time. Since I didn't know Cutler, I assumed he was one of the Houstonites.

"I didn't mean to hit you cold like this," Crosse said, "but it is good news. We're prepared to pay cash."

He'd hit me cold in more than one way. Crosse was likable, but I had doubts as to his integrity because I believed Zanjiv Mehendru had doubted him.

He talked on, managing to be both ingratiating and aggressive. I listened, half out of curiosity at hearing what he had to say, half from surprise at finding myself in such a situation. I let him run down, and ended it by telling him it was Clay's decision. Crosse was still trying to get me to commit to convincing Clay to sell as I stood up to indicate that the conversation was ended.

"I doubt Clay will reach any decision about selling until his current problems are resolved," I said, turning toward the door to show him out.

Crosse made no move to get up. "From what I understand of the legal system over there, a substantial amount of cash in the right pocket would make the prosecution go away. Think about it." He stood, walked to the telephone on the counter, ripped a page off the notepad, took a pen from his pocket, and wrote. Straightening, he handed the page to me. "My name and number, so you won't forget." He smiled. "Don't wait too long. The magistrate's ruling will come soon enough and the man really seems to have made up his mind, doesn't he?"

FORTY

Monday, June 10

From Marfa it is twenty-one miles on Highway 17 north to Fort Davis. I made the drive under scudding clouds that promised no rain.

Fort Davis is smaller than Marfa, if you don't count the development outside of town amid the emory oaks and piñon pines that grow in the Davis Mountains. The original fort, the mountains, and the county were named after Jefferson Davis, president of the Confederacy in the 1850s, when he was Secretary of War for the United States. At 5,050 feet, Fort Davis is the highest town in Texas.

The rented office of Bonis Avidus was located on the short Main Street, in a tiny space next to the old drugstore. I parked on the square and walked the short distance. A green Toyota pickup was parked in front of the office. Hugger had said the woman who came to see him about his land drove "one of those little bitty Toyota pickups." I'd been right in guessing she was Christiana Jacobs.

I walked in. The office was a long, deep room with yellow walls. Christiana Jacobs sat at a glass-topped desk in front of the latest in computers. Everything about her looked brittle, as if she would shatter on contact. She had a small round head accentuated by a frizz of dry brown hair and a disproportionately long neck. Her smile, when I introduced myself, was small and tight, as if her skin lacked the elasticity to stretch.

I took the chair in front of the desk. At my right were the wall and the front window onto the street. Beneath the window was a narrow bench with precise stacks of Bonis Avidus brochures.

"Before we talk about your land," Jacobs said, "may I tell you a little about what we do, our goals?"

"I'd like to hear that," I said.

"We're all about saving the land and the native animals and plants that make up our precious heritage. Our goal is to preserve green space for all time and all generations. To achieve this, we hold conservation easements in perpetuity. That means Bonis Avidus will have oversight on the use of the land forever, ensuring that future owners comply with the restrictions for land use." She peered at me and, as if she seemed to expect some response. I nodded.

Satisfied I was paying attention, she went on. "The restrictions mean that the land may not be subdivided, either by sale or gift. For example, an owner can't give a friend five acres to put a camper on. We require the landowner to erect fencing that doesn't interfere with the migration of pronghorn antelope. All improvements to the property—house, barns—have to be contained within twenty-five acres—say you have as little as one section of land, then six hundred and fifteen of those acres must remain untouched. The conservation easement precludes the commercial sale of water from the property. All exterior lighting must—"

"What did you say about the sale of water?" I said.

"The water rights are restricted to the landowner's use and protected from commercial exploitation. That's to prevent a landowner from selling subsurface water rights. The conservation easement is designed and intended to protect the flora and fauna. It's the living things that make the land unique. Water is the key to wildlife survival. There are those people out there who look at water, not as a source of life, but as just another commodity to sell to the highest bidder."

I thought of True Jackson, out of business because of lack of water. And all the growers downstream in the valley.

Christiana Jacobs didn't pause for breath. "I have reports I can show you of wealthy businessmen buying water rights under farms and ranches near Lubbock, Midland, and other places. They have plans and maps of pipelines intended to harvest the water for cities as far away as San Antonio and Fort Worth. These are people ready to exploit a dwindling water supply to the detriment of the environment."

I leaned forward in my chair. "So if someone wanted to sell water, say, to El Paso, the way the rancher in Hudspeth County did, they couldn't?"

"They could not," she said, looking as if the very idea angered her. "The terms of the easement contract are clear and absolute. It's the pumping of groundwater for urban landscaping and agriculture that lowers the water table and sucks rivers dry. Just look at the Rio Grande. Do you know that it no longer flows into the Gulf of Mexico? The mouth of the river is one big sandbar. The river is dying of thirst!"

I gave her a moment to reinstate calm before asking if the restrictions were ever negotiable.

"Never," she said on a quieter note. I could see her pulling in her zealousness and aiming for persuasion. She rose and picked up one of the brochures. Opening it on the desk facing me, she pointed to a pie chart of the organization's land holdings. "As you can see," she said, "seventy-eight percent of the land we have oversight on comes to us as donations, from private landowners and corporations. If you give Bonis Avidus a conservation easement, you can preserve your land in its natural state for all time."

"I thought you bought land?" I said.

"Any land we buy must be very special."

"You bought Jip Jackson's ranch, didn't you?"

"We did, but such purchases are rare. In that case, the price was low and the land was suitable for restricted development, which means we retain all the easement rights while allowing a small number of new owners to live on the land. By dividing it, we increased our revenue for overseeing the easements we have. I doubt whether our California headquarters would allow us to make another purchase so soon."

"Sorry," I said, rising from the chair. "I guess I misunderstood. I thought Crosse Hickman said Bonis Avidus wanted to buy my property."

"Crosse Hickman!" Her face flushed a mottled red. "That young man no longer works for this office and I can't imagine why he let you think he did. He was fired over a month ago for using contacts gained through Bonis Avidus to acquire land for another group, property that we'd been working on to have donated to us."

I sat down again. "What other group?"

"A private company out of Chihuahua City," she said. "Grupo Prima, it's called. Back in May they announced plans for what they called the Cross-Border Nature Preserve Project, to be owned and controlled entirely by them. They have admirable goals, seemingly, but so far all we have is their word that they're going to do what they say—create an extensive eco-region. They buy land outright. Once they own it, they can do what they like. Develop it, resell it, anything."

I had to control the tremor in my voice as I asked her my next question. "The Mott Ranch, would that have been one of the properties you thought Crosse was trying to acquire for Bonis Avidus?"

"Yes. We'd talked to them extensively about donating a conservation easement. At least, that's what Crosse was supposed to be doing. Instead, he made an offer for Grupo Prima. I was shocked when the Motts told me who they'd sold to. Because of Crosse's treachery, we lost the Picket Ranch, too. Almost one hundred thousand acres in two purchases. It would have been a huge acquisition for any environmental group. I can only hope Grupo Prima's Cross-Border Nature Preserve will have the same strict controls we provide."

"If I wanted to find out more about this Cross-Border Nature Preserve, who would I ask?"

"For an objective opinion," Christiana Jacobs said, "Carlo Rojo in Ojinaga. He's with Agrupación Ecologisto. They've been pressing for preservation of some portion of the Chihuahuan Desert in Mexico for years."

She scribbled something on a notepad, tore off the sheet, and leaned over the desk to give it to me. "His office address and telephone number," she said. "I hope, after you talk with him, you'll decide Bonis Avidus is the better answer for your land than selling." She came around from behind the desk and walked over to the bench, picked up one of the brochures, and handed it to me. "Maybe this will help you decide."

FORTY-ONE

Wednesday, June 12

I was on the road to Ojinaga, a long day in front of me. The previous Sunday, a soon as Crosse had left, I'd telephoned Lucy Ramos, the postmistress, and asked her if she could open up long enough for me to clear my box in the tiny front room of her house that serves as our post office. In ten minutes, I had a solitary envelope, addressed to Clay Jones, out of the box, and tore it open.

A cover letter bearing my name explained that the writer understood Clay was presently being held in Ojinaga, a situation which he hoped would soon be happily resolved. Edmund Cutler asked that I would forward the enclosed letter to Clay with his best wishes:

This is to inform you that the late Canfield Baines bequeathed to you the property known as Choke Canyon Ranch, comprising eleven sections. As a stipulation of Mr. Baines's will, you may inherit only if you are willing and able to provide lifetime care *on the property* for the seven mules owned by Mr. Baines. (Apostle, Monk, Little Jack, Deacon, Jonah, Reader, and Solomon.) Mr. Baines felt that as a veterinarian you would be willing to accept such a responsibility. He could not foresee that, for reasons beyond your control, you might be unable to take possession of the property immediately.

In addition to the property, Mr. Baines set aside certain monies in trust to pay yearly taxes and such maintenance of the property as fencing, etcetera.

I understand that at present you are unable to say whether you can except the stipulation. I have arranged for the care of the livestock for an interim period that is, as of now, indefinite. We must hope that your situation resolves itself. I shall look forward to meeting you at such time as you are able to come to my office.

I had the letter with me, intending to show it to Clay as part of today's errands.

My first stop was at the bakery, where I found Olivia training a new employee. We went to her office.

"Do you know an environmentalist named Carlo Rojo?" I asked, as she offered me coffee from the ever-present pot.

"Yes, Carlo is an old friend."

"Tell me a little about him."

"He's a good man, and a poor one, because he spends the little money he has to pay for pamphlets for schoolchildren about ecology. He helped found the Agrupación Ecologisto chapter here. They've tried for years to get the bureaucrats in Mexico City to do more than support the environment on paper. Carlo isn't only an activist, he has a degree in environmental studies."

"He may be able to give me some information that, indirectly, might help Clay," I said.

"I'll call him and tell him that you're coming as my friend

to see him," Olivia said, reaching for the telephone at the end of the long table where we sat. She dialed and waited, then replaced the receiver with a disgusted noise. "No connection," she said disgustedly. She picked up a pen and wrote a note of introduction instead.

The office of Agrupación Ecologisto was in an old storefront near the plaza. A dusty assortment of ecology-related posters, pamphlets, and books in both Spanish and English were displayed in the windows on either side of the door. Inside, the office had antique file cabinets, a battered desk, a wall of overflowing bookshelves as dusty as the front window, and a very old copy machine in front of which a man knelt, his back to me.

"Señor Rojo?"

"Yes," said an impatient voice as the tall figure unfolded itself to hold up black-smeared hands like a priest giving a benediction. He was thin and balding, with a fine-featured face made studious by reading glasses, the nosepiece mended with electrical tape.

I crossed the room, told him my name, and said Olivia Berrera sent me, as I held out the note. He hesitated to accept it, because of the ink on his hands.

"It won't hurt if it gets dirty," I said.

He took it carefully by an edge with two fingers, read and nodded. "Yes, I see, yes." He looked at me over the glasses. "Excuse me. I must clean my hands." He vanished beyond a door at the back, returning in five minutes, his hands looking scrubbed but still lightly stained. He pulled the only chair in the room around from behind the desk and offered it to me while he perched on the edge of the desk.

"You're interested in our movement?" he said, his light brown eyes intent. There was no hint in either his tone or his face that he recognized my name or associated it in any way with Clay or Zanjiv Mehendru's murder. He was a true zealot, too busy with his own cause to take note of current events, unless they affected his own interests.

"What can you tell me about Grupo Prima's Cross-Border Nature Preserve Project?"

He gave my question some thought, then said guardedly, "May I ask why you're inquiring?"

"I've been approached by someone, a man named Crosse Hickman, about buying some land."

"I don't know anyone by that name," Rojo said, a frown creasing the skin between his eyes.

"According to Christiana Jacobs—"

"I know Christiana."

"She told me that Crosse Hickman works as a kind of land agent for Grupo Prima. If that's correct, Grupo Prima has already bought two large ranches in Presidio County, nearly one hundred thousand acres. Yesterday, Crosse approached me about some land my husband may inherit. Crosse didn't mention Grupo Prima specifically, he just made a reference to 'the nature preserve.' The land he wants to buy from us has a ciénaga on it."

The impatience on Rojo's face vanished, replaced by a fierce look.

"Nothing," he said, "that Grupo Prima does is to anyone's advantage but the Blancas family's. I would not sell them so much as one acre."

"That's clear enough," I said. "But would you tell me why? I don't ask this lightly, I promise you."

Rojo shifted his weight on the desk edge. "Anything I tell you is known by many people—the farmers, the judiciales, the politicians, probably the president of Mexico knows."

"I don't know."

"You know about the water debt Mexico owes your country?"

"The water from the Rio Conchos that Mexico is supposed to release into the Rio Grande as part of the treaty agreement that supplies Mexico with water from the Colorado River."

"Yes. That water is being used for irrigation in the Rio

213

Conchos Basin. Since the government began hoarding the water ten years ago, the amount of farmland around the basin has steadily increased, even with the drought. Some of that water is being used to keep the poppy fields green and productive for the Blancas family's drug empire. Now you tell me Grupo Prima is trying to buy land with water in your country. I tell you that it's not for any good reason."

Rojo stood up and paced in the small space. "This drought exemplifies the calamity toward which we're all headed. Look at Juárez. El Paso supplies nearly all the water Juárez uses and the aquifer they're pumping, the Hueco Bolsom, will be dry no later than 2020. Already we have more people than water. And the same is true for every town along the border. If one country decides not to honor the treaty, the other is left dry. It's as simple as that. Look at what's happened to the Rio Grande. The river is dying, and with it the green belt and the wildlife that depends on it. It's an ecological disaster."

He stopped pacing and stood over me as if to emphasize his next words. "But listen, the treaty between your country and mine covers only surface water. For groundwater, there are no agreements. If Grupo Prima is trying to acquire land with a spring, it's not for any environmental reason. I've suspected the intent of their so-called nature preserve from the beginning. The Blancas family already owns a fifty-two-section ranch abutting the border. If they can buy enough land on the other side, they'll control an open drug corridor."

FORTY-TWO

From Rojo's office, I went straight to El Cereso, arriving just as the gatekeeper was letting in the families. As I got out of the pickup, I could see both Enrique Vera and Warden Martinez standing by the gate, looking anxiously in my direction. I almost ran across the street, a hollow, sick feeling in my stomach, as I brushed past slower-moving visitors to get inside.

"Has something happened to Clay?" I asked, searching their faces for how bad the news might be.

"No, no, señora," the warden assured me.

"The magistrado is holding another hearing this afternoon," Enrique said. "I tried to telephone you this morning to let you know."

"I was here in Ojinaga," I said. "What about Tito Berg? Is he here?"

"He's in court in Chihuahua City," Enrique said, as if announcing a death. "I left word with his secretary, but he won't have time, which is what the magistrado wanted, I imagine."

I lifted my chin, looked him in the eyes, and said, "Then it's a good thing we have you." Relief lit his face, making me glad I'd successfully hidden my doubts.

"Please," the warden said to us, "come inside my office. You have a few minutes before the magistrado arrives at the courtroom. He's slow and lazy, that one, even when he wants to be fast."

"I take it Resendez is acting fast now," I said in a low voice to Enrique as we crossed the prison yard. "Why? What's going on?"

The warden escorted us into his office, pulled out a chair for me, and smiled and nodded his way out.

Enrique turned to me as the door closed and said, "I think the pressure Berg is putting on Vascón and Carmin, plus the negative newspaper coverage, is having its effect. I think Magistrado Resendez is afraid the Sixth District Appeals Court may let Clay go unless the prosecutor produces that videotape."

"But why so abruptly?" I said.

"Fewer reporters."

The door opened and the warden entered with Clay. We didn't get a chance to speak to each other, because immediately behind the warden came a guard, saying, "The magistrado is waiting."

"That's a first," Warden Martinez said.

We followed him down the hall and out the far door into the municipal building. When we entered the courtroom, the only people present were the prosecutor, Alfonso Carmin, Magistrate Resendez—looking sweaty—and the shirt-sleeved clerk, who was rolling a television with a built-in VCR to the front. He positioned it to one side so that the magistrate as well as the lawyers could see it.

Carmin, a videotape in one hand, said, "Magistrado, this is the new evidence we promised, the video of the border crossing taken from the toll booth on this side. It was recorded the night of the murder, as the date on the tape will show. You will see the suspect's vehicle leaving from Ojinaga that night after the time it's believed Zanjiv Mehendru was murdered."

Carmin turned on the set, adjusted it for video, and slid in the tape. There was a blank space and then a series of blurry black-and-white images that I finally realized were vehicles whizzing by. After a few seconds of watching, Enrique was on his feet.

"Magistrado, you can't even read the license numbers! This isn't evidence. It proves nothing!"

Carmin paused the tape, pointing at a light pickup that might have been any make, so lacking in definition was the image. "That's the suspect's pickup, and the time on the tape shows eleven thirty-two." Carmin stopped the tape and removed it without rewinding it. I leaned forward and talked into Enrique's ear.

"The suspect will be returned to prison and a trial date will be set," Resendez said so fast, his words ran together.

"The bridge closes at ten o'clock," Enrique shouted to the magistrate's back as the clerk closed the connecting door. Clay gave a long sigh and put his head in his hands.

I left for home immediately. There was nothing I could say to Clay that would help, least of all that he'd inherited land from Hugger Baines, land he could not claim if he was in prison.

As soon as I got in, I telephoned Christiana Jacobs at the Bonia Avidus office in Fort Davis. "If Grupo Prima wanted to sell water in large quantities, what steps would they have to take?" I asked, after identifying myself.

"They'd have to apply to the Far West Texas Water Conservation District for a high-impact water permit. Are you saying they're going to do this?"

"I don't know yet."

"If they've applied, it's public record," Christiana Jacobs said.

I hung up, got the area-wide telephone book, looked under "Government Offices," and punched in the number. I outlined the information I needed. The clerk excused herself to look at the permit requests.

"Are you there?" she asked when she came back to the telephone.

"Yes."

"Grupo Prima, under the name of the Cross-Border Nature Preserve Project, has applied twelve days ago for a high-impact water permit for property owned in Presidio County."

"What does that mean exactly, 'high impact'?"

"Let's see," she said. "Here it is. They requested permission to pump a maximum of ten million gallons per year for a period of time no less than ten years."

FORTY-THREE

Friday, June 14

After closing on Friday evening, while I was in the front room restocking shelves, someone knocked. Through the glass I saw Jack Raff and unlocked the door.

He came in bearing a full bottle of Teachers whiskey. We went through to the back, where he flopped into the chair like an exhausted spaniel. His dress was formal, for him, which meant jeans rather than shorts, a shirt rather than a T-shirt, and tennis shoes rather than sandals.

"I thought you might want a bit of company and a bit of this bottle."

I opened the whiskey and filled two glasses. "Let's sit on the porch. I have a lot to tell you."

I explained about the prisoner named Rivera who was watching and reporting on the effect of prison on Clay, about Zanjiv Mehendru's interest in Crosse Hickman's efforts to persuade the ranchers to sell, about the Mott and Picket ranches having been sold to Grupo Prima, about what I'd learned about Crosse Hickman from Christiana Jacobs, about what Carlo Rojo had said about Grupo Prima's Cross-Border Nature Preserve Project, about Hugger's will and Crosse Hickman's approach to me about buying the land, and about Grupo Prima's water-permit request.

Last, I told him what I believed about the circumstances that led to the murder of Zanjiv Mehendru. "The first year out here, Crosse rented a house in Presidio, but he spent most of his time on the other side. 'Traveling,' he told everyone. That has to have been when he hooked up with the Blancases. Maybe he uses drugs or is a small-time dealer and they keep him supplied. Maybe their attraction was simply their wealth and power. I think Crosse's job with Bonis Avidus was genuine for a few months, until somehow he found out what was in the hydrologist's report. His friendship with Daniel probably provided the opportunity, especially if Mehendru took the report home with him and kept it in his office there. Based on Grupo Prima's applying to pump ten million gallons of water a year, I'd say it's a sure thing that the report shows a major aquifer under the two big ranches Grupo Prima has already bought. I think Crosse took the information about the report to his friends the Blancases and landed himself a job as their land man, buying water-rich ranches in a water-starved area. And all before the landowners knew what they might be sitting on. That's when the idea of the Cross-Border Nature Preserve Project was born. Hang an environmental tag on it and who's going to speak against it? All it took to legitimize it was publicity, so they held a press conference."

"And Zanjiv Mehendru found out the truth," Jack said.

"Enough of it to get him killed. I think Hugger died because he wouldn't let them have the most important piece of land."

"They gambled that his heirs would sell?" Jack said.

"Crosse told me he knew Hugger had no relatives . . . I

don't even like to think about it." I took a deep drink of the whiskey and felt the revitalizing warmth sliding down my throat.

"You'll be better for talking it through," Jack said.

"After Mehendru died," I said slowly, "and the publicity about his murder didn't, the attorney general of Chihuahua might have felt he had to make an arrest of someone. Anybody would have done for a scapegoat, but what if the Blancases found out Clay would inherit Choke Canyon and decided to use that knowledge to get the land? Kate Worthy told me Crosse was aggressively persistent in trying to buy her ranch. I found out just how aggressive when he came here. The only way Crosse could have known that Clay would inherit Choke Canyon was if Hugger told him. I think Crosse pushed Hugger too hard about buying his place and Hugger tried to get rid of Crosse by saying its future was taken care of, like the mules, because it would go to Clay. And Crosse dutifully reported that to the Blancases."

"So they set Clay up," Jack said. "That explains the extremes to which the state police and prosecutor have gone to keep him in prison."

"The last thing Crosse said to me was that the money for Choke Canyon could buy Clay's freedom. Rather sinister, now that I know who his masters are."

It was a while before either of us spoke again. The sun was setting, turning the mountains to flame and shadow. We sat and watched the light fade to lavender, then turn to night.

"I want to know where Daniel Mehendru stands in all this." In the dark, my voice sounded unnaturally loud. "The last thing Zanjiv Mehendru wanted, according to Mercedes Solar, would have been for Daniel to have anything to do with the Blancas family." I told Jack about my visit to the Sloe Ranch and finding Kim Blancas de Garza there with Daniel. "Daniel admires the Blancases. I don't know what they told him about Zanjiv Mehendru's break with the family, but whatever it was convinced him to hide his relationship with them, at least at first."

"And if his father found out?"

"Daniel sounded bitter when he spoke about what he called his father's 'desertion' of Daniel's grandmother. I think he might have confronted his father after the grandmother died."

"I gather Mehendru was the kind of father who doesn't explain his reasons," Jack said. "He'd simply expect Daniel to obey his wishes."

And of course, Daniel didn't," I said. "If Zanjiv Mehendru knew his son was entangled with the Blancas family, it would have been one more powerful reason to denounce what he suspected they were planning by buying local land. No one knew what they were capable of better than he."

We speculated for some time about whether it might have been Daniel who told the Blancases about the hydrologist's report.

"If he did," Jack said, "he was showing off, trying to prove to them he could be helpful. He's immature and he lacks self-confidence, so he's malleable."

"He is also lonely. The Blancases provide an instant family, tell him he's wonderful, convince him he's loved. Daniel buys into the nature-preserve project as a reality. He wants to do something to show his new family he's on their side."

"So he gives them the map," Jack said sadly.

"Maybe that's how the Blancases planned it. They could have found out Mehendru was on the Tri-County Water Planning Board and that a report was in the works from the newspaper. Maybe they cultivated Daniel so they'd be in a position to ask for information. His father was out of the house from Monday through Friday. I would assume any water-board papers would have been kept there in his desk. Easy enough for Daniel to find them and pass them on."

"Or for his friend Crosse."

We left it at that. Undecided. Daniel as victim or victimizer. Of Crosse, I had no doubt. He was a villain.

Jack left soon after. I locked up and went to the register, where underneath the cash drawer I kept important bits of information. I removed the slip on which Crosse had written his name and number and carried it with me to the porch. I sipped the last of my whiskey and starred at his signature. I'd told Jack all the facts I knew. What I hadn't told him was the cold hate I felt for the people doing this to Clay.

FORTY-FOUR

Saturday, June 15

In the morning, between waiting on customers, I assembled everything I would need—the notes I'd copied from Grupo Prima's Web site, the Bonis Avidus brochure Christiana Jacobs had insisted I take—and sat at my desk to compose the first draft of a document. Getting details right took time, and the wastebasket in the corner overflowed with crumpled sheets of paper before I was satisfied with the result.

When I'd finished, I telephoned Eddie Salaman, editor of the *International,* who'd introduced me to Angel Girón after Clay's first hearing. I asked him for a list of fax numbers. He had three at hand, and promised to call back within the hour with the others.

After lunch, I went out to the clinic, where Mike was feeding the baby emu. Squib, the now fledged Inca dove, was on his shoulder. I typed the document I'd composed on Clay's old machine, then returned to the trading post for the item that was key to my plan, the slip of paper on which Crosse Hickman had written his name and address. I propped it in front of me at my desk, and for nearly an hour, I practiced his signature. A dozen sheets of lined notebook paper later, I decided my career as a forger was doomed.

I went to the bedroom, rummaged in a drawer until I found a sheet of white tissue paper folded around a never-worn scarf Claudia had given me on my birthday in January. I fetched a new pencil from the school supplies I sell, returned to my desk, placed the single thin sheet of semi-transparent tissue over Crosse's signature, and carefully traced it.

Turning the tracing over, I used the side of the pencil lead to blacken the back. Removing the letter I'd typed from the desk drawer, I placed it flat and positioned the tissue with the traced signature over it. A small amount of Scotch tape held it in place as I went over the signature firmly enough to transfer it to the page below.

I lifted the tape and removed the tracing, then went over the signature with a black-ink ballpoint. The finished letter, now with Crosse Hickman's signature in ink at the bottom, was good enough. After all, I didn't have to fool Crosse, only make him think I could fool others, and thus precipitate him into action.

By late afternoon, I was back at my desk, writing down everything Jack and I had gone over, in the order of occurrence—a time line. When it was done, I called Dennis Busta-mante, catching him just as he came home from the five-o'clock mass I knew he attended at Santa Teresa de Jesús.

We talked for a long time. After we disconnected, I faxed him the time line, my notes on Grupo Prima, Zanjiv Mehen-dru's obituary, a copy of the document I'd created, every scrap of information I had.

At seven-thirty, Dennis called back. "Make the appointment," he said.

I hung up and punched in the home telephone number for Crosse Hickman. He answered on the fourth ring.

"I talked it over with Clay," I told Crosse without preamble. "He's willing to sell Choke Canyon. I'd like to come to your house on Tuesday at ten to talk over the details and draw up a contract. Clay's defense lawyer thinks what you told me about using the money to get him out of jail is a good idea."

"I can guarantee it will do the trick," Crosse said. "See you Tuesday."

I called Dennis back and confirmed. "Tuesday at ten."

"I'll be in front of his house," Dennis said.

That evening, while the Movie Night kids cheered on the Cisco Kidd and his sidekick Pancho, I sat in the darkened corner of the front room and worried that the plan might fail.

FORTY-FIVE

Tuesday, June 18

I closed the trading post at nine-thirty. At five minutes to ten, filled with cold resolve, I stood before the public fax machine in the front room. The letter I'd written over Crosse Hickman's signature was on the table beside the machine, ready to send to his personal fax number, the one I'd found listed in the Bonis Avidus brochure.

I watched the clock. At one minute to ten, I lifted the receiver and dialed Crosse Hickman's home telephone.

"This is Texana Jones."

"I hope for your husband's sake you haven't changed your mind about selling Choke Canyon," he said, threat vibrating in his voice.

"I'm sending a document to your fax number. Unless you call me back at this number in five minutes, I'm prepared to fax the same document to the news media listed at the top."

I hung up, inserted the page, put the fax on "speaker," and punched in the number. Crosse's machine rang twice, then the fax tone sounded. I hit "send."

As the page ran out of my machine, I picked it up, judging the length of time it would take Crosse to read it by doing the same myself.

FROM: Crosse Hickman
    211 Candelaria St.
    Presidio, TX.

TO: *La Voz de Ojinaga* 145-472-87
  El Diario de Chihuahua 14-666-7848
  El Jornada 705-05-50
  Televisa 705-98-74
  The Presidio *International* 915-229-0050
  The El Paso *Times* 915-555-5335

RE: Crupo Prima and the Cross-Border Nature Preserve Project

As an employee of Grupo Prima and CEO Arturo Blancas, I've negotiated land purchases totaling nearly one hundred thousand acres in Presidio County, Texas, for Grupo Prima under the guise of putting together a nature preserve. The choice of the land in question was based on data in a hydrologist's report commissioned by the Tri-County Water Planning Board and stolen from Zanjiv Mehendru, one of the board members. That report, not yet made public, shows an aquifer of vast proportions beneath the land which Grupo Prima bought. Zanjiv Mehendru, the head of the International Water and Boundary Commission who last February was shot execution-style in Ojinaga, discovered the truth about the so-called Cross-Border Nature Preserve Project and intended to denounce Grupo Prima and the Blancas family. I am meeting with the authorities to provide proof that Zanjiv Mehendru was assassinated on orders of Aurelio Blancas, known to have ties to one of the largest drug cartels in Chihuahua State. The Blancas family then arranged with the judiciales and the Chihuahua State Attorney General to have an innocent man arrested and held for the murder in order to force the sale of one parcel of land vital to the Blancases' gaining control of the largest underground aquifer in the Far West Texas region. You may verify Grupo Prima's real intent for this land by checking with the Far West Texas Water Conservation District. Grupo Prima has applied for a high-impact pumping permit for up to 10 million gallons of water per year. I am providing this information to media sources because I now fear for my own life.

Allowing for a couple of minutes of disbelief, I thought Crosse would make the call with time to spare. He did.

"No newspaper in Mexico will follow up on this," he shouted. "The reporters and editors know what would happen to them."

"I think they might surprise you. All it takes is one. *La Voz de Ojinaga,* for instance. The editor has taken a personal interest in this case. Or a call from an El Paso *Times* reporter, asking the Blancas family for an interview about certain allegations to do with their environmental project."

"Any reporter would call me first and I'll deny it."

"You won't deny anything. You'll be dead. You know what they say, narcotraficantes only recognize one commandment: 'Thou shalt not rat.' Did I mention I intend to send the first fax to Grupo Prima headquarters, the office of the president, Arturo Blancas? Shall I read you his fax number? I'm sure you know it by heart."

"Bitch! I'll kill you!"

"I don't like your tone," I said, hanging up.

Immediately, I punched in my father's number to tell him I had hopes that Clay would be exonerated soon. We talked for about fifteen minutes, more than long enough for Crosse, hearing the busy signal, to think I was sending the faxes.

A few minutes after I said good-bye to my father, Dennis Bustamante telephoned our private number.

"Hickman is locked in the back of the sheriff's car. He came running out of the house, took one look at me, and bolted for his Volvo. I yelled 'Stop'; he kept going. He was halfway in the front seat when I grabbed him around the waist and he went for the gun he had tucked into the waistband of his pants. Assaulting a sheriff's deputy with a deadly weapon ought to hold him."

FORTY-SIX

Friday, June 21

I pressed the receiver to my ear and placed a finger in the other to hear Dennis Bustamante's voice on the telephone while frantically signaling the teenager walking the aisles to turn down the boom box he'd brought into the trading post.

"We matched the prints at the ciénaga to a pair of boots in Hickman's closet," the deputy said. "We found bloodstains on a shirt that we expect to match to Hugger's. When we searched his desk we found a copy of a map marked 'Igneous Aquifer.' Mack Friedel identified it as a page from the hydrologist's report. Friedel said he'd personally numbered the copies handed out to the water-board members. The number on Hickman's copy was the number of the report that went to Zanjiv Mehendru."

"Did Crosse say how he got it?"

"He dribbled information like it would choke him if he didn't get it out," Dennis said. "Daniel Mehendru copied the whole report and gave it to his uncle, Arturo Blancas, last January, within two days after his father brought the original home to study. Blancas passed the map page on to Hickman with instructions about which properties to buy."

"What made Zanjiv Mehendru suspicious enough to go asking questions at the ranches?"

"He noticed that things in his desk had been disturbed, asked the son; the kid lost his temper and bragged about what he'd done."

"So Mehendru had more reason than Grupo Prima's crooked land deals to publically discredit the Blancases," I said. "He'd have wanted to keep them away from his son."

"I'm going this afternoon to have a talk with Daniel."

"His punishment will be living with the knowledge that his action resulted in his father's death. Dennis, what about—"

"Hickman practically begged the district attorney to let him admit to killing Mehendru in return for a plea bargain in Hugger's murder. The DA agreed not to seek the death penalty and promised to oppose Hickman's extradition to Mexico if the authorities in Chihuahua request it. He faxed a copy of Hickman's confession to Attorney General Benito Vascón and to Tito Berg."

"Thank you, Dennis. Thank you so much."

"Hey, anytime. You did the footwork."

I hung up, shooed out the teenager with the boom box, locked up, and headed for Ojinaga. I had a feeling that when I told Warden Martinez what had happend, he'd let me see Clay even though it wasn't a family day.

The following day, Enrique Vera came to the trading post to tell me that Tito Berg had personally carried copies of Crosse Hickman's confession to the judiciales headquarters in Chihuahua, to prosecutor Alfonso Carmin, and to the Sixth District Appeals Court magistrate, Antonia de Juana.

I personally leaked the story of Crosse Hickman's confession to every newspaper listed on the bogus fax.

FORTY-SEVEN

Thursday, July 11

It was three-forty. Clay and I sat in the warden's office with Olivia and Mario Berrera, Howard Barton, and Jack Raff. We'd been there since eleven that morning, in anticipation of an appellate ruling that had yet to arrive.

I held on fiercely to Clay's hand and watched hope ebb from his face. At four, we'd been told, the court would close for the day. Tomorrow, the entire court system would shut down for a two-week vacation.

At three minutes to four, a shout went up from the direction of the municipal compound. Running feet pounded in the hallway and Enrique Vera appeared at the open door, waving a sheet of paper, his face triumphant.

"You're free!" he said, handing the warden a copy of the Sixth District Appeals Court's order to release Clay.

Warden Martinez shook Clay's hand. "Pack your things."

"I'm wearing what I'm taking home," Clay told him. "You can give the cot and chairs and fan to one of the prisoners."

The warden opened his desk drawer, removed the set of keys to the vetmobile, and held them out to Clay. "Your company and your services as a veterinarian have been much appreciated."

"I'll see you for Zapata's yearly checkup," Clay said, bending to stroke the cat, who'd sought safety under the desk when Enrique burst in.

I had ridden with Jack so I could go home with Clay in the vetmobile. The warden escorted us down the hallway and out into the compound to the clapping of the guards. Shouts of congratulation rose over the wall of the prison yard as word spread of Clay's release.

Clay drove. At the end of the bridge, we stopped for customs. With a wide smile, the uniformed agent leaned down to the driver's open window and asked, as he did hundreds of times a day of those crossing over, "Your nationality, sir?"

"American citizen," Clay answered.

"Welcome home," the agent said, and waved us on our way.

EPILOGUE

Two days before Clay's release, the Presidio *International* carried a front-page story:

The Tri-County Water Planning Board has released a report that will have a profound effect on land values in the region. The study by an independent hydrologist indicates that a large portion of Presidio County sits atop an aquifer, dubbed the "Igneous Aquifer," that is easily one of the most important groundwater reservoirs in the region. According to the study, made by Saga Technologies, the aquifer may cover as much as fifteen hundred square miles and perhaps contain as much as 100 million acre-feet of water, explained Board Chairman Mack Friedel. It is believed it may extend over the border into Chihuahua State, Mexico. "We don't have a lot of evidence to prove it," Friedel said, "but it appears to be one big aquifer. The hydrologist added up proven wells, bolsons, and springs.

He believes the data indicates a massive amount of water over a widespread area. This is good news for us all."

On August 9, the *Presidio International* ran this story:

The hydrologist who discovered and named the short-lived Igneous Aquifer was nowhere to be found when geologists, environmentalists, and others held a public forum at Sul Ross State University to discuss his findings as reported to the Tri-County Water Planning Board. After careful study of the hydrologist's report, local experts from Sul Ross said there was nothing in the study to justify the assumption that groundwater under Presidio County was either connected or abundant. Their position is based on the fact that the rock in the area is highly fractured, making accurate prediction of where water may be found impossible. "Hydrology is, at best, a very inexact science. The so-called Igneous Aquifer doesn't exist," explained one geologist. "If the board had consulted us, we could have told them that." "The water board has wasted money that could have been better spent on environmental impact studies of the Rio Grande as a vanished water resource," said Christiana Jacobs, director of the local chapter of Bonis Avidus, a nonprofit environmental group.

Afterword

The details in this book concerning the 1944 bilateral treaty between the United States and Mexico and that country's failure to honor the treaty are true. In June 2002, Mexico promised to release ninety thousand acre-feet as a token of its debt; at the same time, Mexico's congress passed a resolution calling the debt "fictional." As of March 2003 no water has been released.

The furor over the short-lived "Igneous Aquifer" in far west Texas is true, as is the interest of private investors in buying huge ranches solely to obtain valuable underground water rights.

Texas presently has the second-largest population growth in the United States. Statewide, demand for water is predicted to outstrip available water resources by no later than 2050. Exacerbated by what the El Paso *Herald Post* called "the worst drought in over half a century" in northern Mexico and far west Texas, the situation along the Rio Grande border is more immediately dire. The urban complex of El Paso–Ciudad Juárez is one example. The urban complex does not have enough water for current populations. As *El Continental* of Ciudad Juárez put it, "The lack of water is frightening." Hueco Tanks, the source of sixty percent of El Paso's water supply, is predicted to run dry no later than 2020. The El Paso water utility plans to pipe as much as fifty thousand acre-feet per year from ranches it bought in Presidio, Jeff Davis, and Culberson counties, a figure that does not meet projected needs. As Ramón Eduardo Ruiz puts it in *On the Rim of Mexico*, "Water, [in the borderland] more and more, becomes an issue of life and death for one and all, whether American or Mexican."